MATTHEW'S
RISE

MATTHEW'S RISE

DEBRA SPEARMAN

PELICAN PUBLISHING
NEW ORLEANS 2021

The word "Pelican" and the depiction of a pelican are trademarks of Arcadia Publishing Company Inc. and are registered in the U.S. Patent and Trademark Office.

Library of Congress Cataloging-in-Publication Data

Names: Spearman, Debra, 1954- author.
Title: Matthew's rise / Debra Spearman.
Description: New Orleans : Pelican Publishing, 2021. | Audience: Ages 8-12. | Audience: Grades 4-6. | Summary: "In this middle-reader novel set on Caddo Lake in northwest Louisiana, eleven-year-old Matthew Morin and his friends investigate a suspicious fire and, in the process, discover a Caddo Indian mound. They soon turn their attention to the enigmatic new neighbor down the road. As they investigate further, they are pitched into a race against time to save the site from desecration"— Provided by publisher.
Identifiers: LCCN 2019056875 | ISBN 9781455625444 (paperback) | ISBN 9781455625451 (ebook)
Subjects: LCSH: Caddo Indians—Louisiana—Juvenile fiction. | CYAC: Caddo Indians—Fiction. | Indians of North America—Louisiana—Fiction. | Mounds--Fiction. | Cemeteries—Fiction. | Indians of North America—Funeral customs and rites—Fiction. | Caddo Lake Region (La. and Tex.)—Fiction. | Louisiana—Antiquities—Fiction.
Classification: LCC PZ7.1.S714 Mat 2021 | DDC [Fic]—dc23
LC record available at https://lccn.loc.gov/2019056875

Printed in the United States of America
Published by Pelican Publishing
New Orleans, LA
www.pelicanpub.com

To my family for their belief in me

CHAPTER 1

MONDAY, JUNE 9

With outstretched wings the hawk glided onto the power line above the Morins' SUV. Staring out the window, Matthew caught a glimpse of the bird as his mom drove down the black-top road toward the old family farmhouse. He and his dad had always watched for the hawk when they came for a stay at the house. With tears stinging his eyes, Matthew furtively wiped his nose with his face turned toward the window. He didn't want Mom or Kate to see him crying.

The familiar scene flew past the window. The pasture lay to the left of the road and the pine woods lined the right. In the blur of the pine trees, Matthew glimpsed something in the woods. He jerked his head around to look. Who or what could be out here? They were at least fifteen minutes from town. There were only two houses on this road—the Stewards' and his family's farmhouse. Why would Mr. Charlie be in the woods on this side of the road when his house is on the other side?

"Whatcha looking at?" asked Kate, also turning in the back seat to look at the woods behind them.

"Nothing, I guess."

Matthew's gaze returned to the front as a clearing in the trees revealed the yard and the white farmhouse. The tires on the cattle guard sounded strangely hollow as the SUV pulled through the gap in the barbed-wire fence. Caddo Lake was visible down the hill behind the house. Dad had once described the big lake as "meandering" around the hills of northwest Louisiana and east Texas, including the hill their house sat on.

A fine cloud of dust flew up from the dirt drive in front of the farmhouse as Mom slowed the SUV. Matthew stepped out onto the old brick walk that was almost buried under the dirt and grass that led toward the porch. Why didn't this walkway line up with the brick steps of the front porch? He wished he had asked Dad about it.

"Look, the lantanas are in bloom," Mom said, referring to the yellow flowers on each side of the front steps. "I'm glad to see that Charlie has been down to mow the grass. I hope he has primed the pump."

"I could have done that, Mom," Matthew said. He and Dad had primed the pump behind the house many times. Since his dad's parents and grandparents were no longer alive, the house wasn't occupied very often. Glancing toward the pump house, he spied an orange bucket at the corner of the house. "What's that big bucket doing beside the flowers?"

"I don't know. I don't remember it."

"We haven't been here since . . . well, in months. I didn't know we had a bucket like that." He stood with furrowed brows, looking at the bucket.

"Maybe it's Charlie's. He was probably watering the flowers." Mom circled to the back of the SUV, pushing on the remote control to open the back gate.

"Hey, Mom," said Kate, climbing out of the back seat, "can I go down to the dock? Please, please . . ."

"Not until we get the car unloaded." A grocery sack fell to the ground as the back gate rose. "Kate, grab that sack. Matthew, go put that bucket in the pump house. I'll hand you the key through the back door." He headed across the grass to the bucket sitting in front of the nandina bushes at the side of the house.

"I don't think Mr. Charlie used this for watering," Matthew said, picking up the bucket. "It's got dirt in the bottom of it."

He looked up, but Mom was already inside.

"Matthew, here's the key," he heard her call from the back door.

Going around the house to the back door, Matthew grabbed the key and walked around the side of the small pump house. The pump house and the house were covered with the same white asbestos tile that was so popular in the 1940s. Dad had warned him about ever damaging the tiles. He unlocked the pad lock, flipped open the hasp, and yanked. The old wooden slat door scraped on the concrete threshold. He leaned in and placed the orange bucket on the concrete floor of the pump house, closed and locked the door, and went back to the front yard. Mom would expect him to help unload the SUV.

After lugging the suitcases and groceries into the house, he and Kate headed down the hill toward the dock. The water of Caddo Lake behind their farmhouse was calm and smelled of fish. "You know, Kate, Dad always said that our great-great-grandparents were lucky to have gotten this land on the lake. Most farmers have to dig ponds for their cattle." Matthew picked up a stick and flung it into the water. Kate followed suit. A large crow flew across the lake into the cypress trees on the other side.

On the lake were two people in a fishing boat, even though this was an inlet and fishermen usually fished in the main channel of the lake. One of them cast a line into the water.

"They're out late for fishing," Matthew mumbled.

"What'd you say?" asked Kate.

"Nothing," replied Matthew. He watched one of the fishermen reach up to pull his cap down lower over his forehead. The sun must be reflecting off the lake into his eyes.

Sitting down on the wooden planks of the dock, Matthew remembered two years ago when he, Dad, and Uncle Roy rebuilt a rotten section. Dad said that they should take advantage of the low water from the lake drawdown. Their days at the farmhouse always seemed to include some work on the property, but Matthew didn't really mind. He liked helping his dad. What would he do now? Once again tears sprang to his eyes. He jumped up and told Kate, "I'll race you to the fence by the woods," starting out without her.

"No fair, Matt. You're getting a head start!" Kate yelled from behind him.

After lunch, Mom was determined to clean the front porch. "I need your help," she told a whining Kate. "The three of us have to stick together." Matthew regarded the serious look on Mom's face and wished that he could take away her concern. He headed through the living room toward the porch, strumming his fingers across the keys of the old upright piano as he walked by it.

When Kate came onto the porch, he laughed at her blond curls poking out from below an old red bandana.

"Don't laugh at me, Matt," Kate said, pouting a little.

"Actually, you look kinda cute," Matthew said, and her pout turned into a smile.

Mom came out, carrying the broom and also sporting a bandana, a navy blue one, over her short, brown hair.

"I remember reading that dirt daubers don't make nests if a ceiling is painted blue," Mom said, swinging the broom at the nests on the ceiling of the porch. Matthew and Kate both ducked as a large section of hardened mud came loose and flew toward them. "That'll be a good first project for us—painting this ceiling before it gets any hotter. And," she added, looking at the old light fixture, "maybe adding a ceiling fan as well." Matthew eyed Kate and they both frowned. Painting did not sound like fun.

With the sweeping finished, Matthew pulled the heavy

porch swing out the front door from the living room. Kate and his mom teamed up to bring out the rocking chairs. Getting the chains of the porch swing onto the hooks in the ceiling was difficult. Mom and Kate tried to hold up the heavy wooden swing while Matthew, standing on a chair, attempted for a second time to slip a chain link onto one of the hooks. Kate's hands slipped, and she jumped back as her end of the swing thumped to the floor.

"Oww."

"Are you okay?" asked Mom, setting down her end.

"It hit my arm," Kate said, rubbing the scraped place with tears in her eyes.

"You almost knocked me off this chair," said Matthew.

"It's too heavy for her. She's only seven," said Mom, walking around the swing to check on Kate.

As he was getting down from the chair, Matthew saw the blue truck pull into the drive. "It's Mr. Charlie," he said.

"Thank goodness," Mom said. She pulled the bandana off her hair. Kate did the same.

Matthew had noticed the blue truck at his house when they passed by earlier and knew Mr. Charlie would come down soon. Mr. Charlie had been forced to retire when the paper mill closed down a couple of years ago. Dad always seemed to appreciate the time Mr. Charlie put into watching over their old family place. It was convenient that he lived so close.

"How are y'all doing?" Mr. Charlie said as he got out of his truck, a purple LSU cap covering his gray hair.

"Hello, Charlie," Mom greeted.

As Mr. Charlie reached over to ruffle Matthew's brown hair, he stopped his hand just above Matthew's head. "Look how tall you've gotten, Matt." He turned to Matthew's mom. "Would you folks like some help? Seems that porch swing is a tad heavy for that little girl." Kate smiled at Mr. Charlie and turned her head to stick her tongue out at Matthew.

"We could use some help with this swing. And thanks for mowing the yard and priming the pump." She looked at him with knitted brows. "I wish you would let me pay you."

"No talk about that, Andrea. If the work gets too much, I'll let you know. I saw you pass the house earlier and thought you might be needin' some help."

"I appreciate that. You are like family to us, Charlie." He smiled at her and nodded his head.

Matthew smiled too, thinking he was getting out of putting up the swing until Mr. Charlie said, "Matt, you go over there and grab that end of the swing and I'll get this end. Andrea, why don't you get on the chair—wait. Hold that thought. I have a ladder in the back of my truck. Matt, come and help me."

As they walked around the back of the truck, Mr. Charlie said, "Matt, jump up there in the back and pick up that end of the ladder. Don't let it scrape the bottom of the truck bed. My truck may be old, but she's my baby." Matthew picked up the end of the ladder, a five-step one like painters use, and walked toward the back of the truck. Mr. Charlie told him, "Prop your end on the tailgate and jump down."

As his feet hit the ground, Matthew turned to look at how clean the truck was except for a little dust from the driveway. Something in the woods to the left of the house caught his eye, but when he looked that way, he didn't see anything.

Probably the hawk.

With the ladder set up on the porch, Mr. Charlie said, "Andrea, why don't you stand on the ladder while Matt and I lift this swing." The chain links were on the hooks in no time. Kate climbed on the swing as her mother stepped off the ladder.

"You want some lemonade, Charlie?" Mom asked. "I think we could use a break."

"I can see how much y'all have been workin' and you just got here," Mr. Charlie said as he surveyed the clean and set-up porch. "I could do with some lemonade, thank you."

Matthew glanced back to the left of the porch, hoping to catch sight of the hawk but still didn't see it. The screen door closed softly as his mother went in to get the lemonade. Glasses and ice clinked from the kitchen.

Mr. Charlie sat in one of the old rocking chairs, and Matthew joined Kate on the porch swing. "I know you kids are glad to be out of school," Mr. Charlie said as he rocked, the wood creaking on the floor boards. Matthew and Kate nodded. "My grandkids sure are. One of them is coming for a visit in a few days."

Mom returned with a tray of glasses and a plate of cookies that she set on a table between the chairs. "Sorry I don't have any of my brownies made yet, Charlie, but maybe these will do."

"These are good by me," Mr. Charlie said as he retrieved two chocolate chip cookies from the plate. "Sarah will be glad to hear y'all are here. She'll want y'all to come down for supper one night."

Mom nodded as she sat in the other rocking chair. "I wanted to thank you again for coming to the funeral. It meant a lot to me and the kids, and I know Dan would have been pleased too." Matthew could see the glistening in his mother's blue eyes. He looked away.

"Wouldn't have it any other way." Mr. Charlie paused, then changed the subject. "These are such good old chairs," he said, patting the arms of the tall-back wooden rocking chair. "Y'all are lucky to have them. Don't make them like this anymore."

"They are due for a revarnishing, I think," Mom said. "I'll have to add that to the list of things to do this summer."

"You plannin' on staying your usual week?" Mr. Charlie asked.

"Maybe for a couple of weeks," she said. "You know, we always had to rush back to town because of Dan's job at the hospital. This year I thought we could stay longer."

Matthew had been planning his strategy for the next

level of his favorite video game and barely listening, but his eyes darted towards his mother when she made that statement. He always enjoyed the week they stayed at the farmhouse, but he wasn't sure how he felt about staying here this year.

He had friends in Shreveport, thirty-five miles south; they all liked to play video games and compare their scores. The extra television and the gaming system were still in Shreveport. Mom said that she thought that he needed a break from it. What was she talking about? He had all the breaks he needed during the school year when his playing time was limited because of homework and practices after school.

He could still hear Dad's voice saying, "One hour on, then two hours off, Matt." How was he going to enjoy the stay at the farmhouse without his dad? Matthew felt that strange pressure welling up in his chest, the same feeling he had felt after the funeral.

He had to get off that porch. He put down his lemonade and, grabbing a cookie, charged down the steps. He headed around the holly tree to the right of the house with no real plan in mind. He pretended not to hear his mom calling after him. He walked toward the old carport that hugged the fence line in the back corner of the yard. Dad had told him that his great-grandfather had built it when he purchased his first car in the 1940s. It was now used for storage.

A toolshed had been built onto the left side of the carport. Matthew aimed for it and opened the wood-slat door. The interior of the space was dark and smelled musty. He moved his hand along the inside wall, feeling for the light switch until he remembered that there was no electricity in the shed.

A noise inside startled him. Out of the corner of his eye, he saw something dark scurry across the floor and out from under a rotten section at the bottom of a board at the back. Matthew jumped out of the shed just in time to see a little raccoon scuttle under the barbed-wire fence and run into the woods. Matthew sighed, then heard a voice. "So you scared that 'coon right out of his hiding place." Matthew looked up to see Mr. Charlie standing behind him.

"Bet you're glad it wasn't a skunk. What's in this old shed, anyway?" Mr. Charlie asked as he ducked his head to step inside. Matthew had come out here to get away from everyone, and now he didn't seem to have a choice but to follow. Dad had always taught him to be respectful of adults. What would Dad have thought if he was rude to Mr. Charlie?

His eyes slowly adjusted to the sunlight sifting through the open doorway and between the wall boards. Old farm tools were hanging on nails along the walls and from the low roof beams. A foot-wide board jutting out from the wall and parallel to the ground served as a work bench. Matthew could see items he recognized, such as an ax, a hammer, and a small wooden toolbox full of screwdrivers. An old jar was filled with screws and washers, and an old coffee can contained nails. Other items, brown with rust, were not familiar.

Mr. Charlie whistled through his teeth. "Look at this. Some of these tools must be from when this was a workin' farm. Wouldn't the pickers love to get their hands on this lot?" He picked up a funny looking shovel. "This is an old potato diggin' rake." He bent to look at a big, heavy-looking piece of wrought iron on the floor beneath the bench. "I think this is a spout from an old sugar cane cooker."

Matthew couldn't help but bend down and look at the piece. "What's a sugar cane cooker?"

"Do you know anything about sugar cane?"

Matthew shook his head.

"Sugar cane was one of the crops raised on farms in this area years ago. You crush the sugar cane stalks in the field to get the juice out. This spout funnels the juice into a pot so it can be boiled into syrup. Then it was put into gallon cans to be sold. Nothing like sugar cane syrup. Ever had any?"

"No," said Matthew. "Does it taste like Aunt Jemima's?"

Mr. Charlie laughed. "So much better. I'll have to get you some."

"How do you know about this, Mr. Charlie? I thought you worked at the paper mill."

"I did. But where I live now was my grandparent's house. They used to farm that land around my house, same as your family farmed the land around this one. I remember the cane syrup that my grandmother made. Nothing better on biscuits."

"You eat syrup on biscuits?" Matthew looked at Mr. Charlie with raised eyebrows.

"You bet. Good on pancakes too. You'll have to try it."

After the unpacking was done, Matthew spent the rest of the day fighting boredom. No video game and no cable television meant nothing to do for entertainment. Matthew knew he had to find something to do. Something more exciting.

Then he remembered the orange bucket. He had forgotten to ask Mr. Charlie about it.

CHAPTER 2

TUESDAY, JUNE 10

The next morning, Matthew thought about the sugar cane syrup as he finished his breakfast of eggs with biscuits and jelly. He planned to go fishing that morning and needed gear. When he walked into the big pantry behind the kitchen to get the gear, Matthew looked at the shelves that ran around three walls of the room. Could this space have been where the cans of cane syrup were stored? He wondered if his dad had ever had any of the cane syrup.

Mom's voice called from the living room. Matthew sighed. Fishing had to be put off. She had more work in store for them. A trip into the nearby town of Vivian to Townsend's Hardware resulted in a can of paint, a paint roller and brush, plastic covers for the rocking chairs and the swing, and a ceiling fan with a light fixture for the porch. They loaded all this into the SUV and headed back to the farmhouse, but not before Matthew and Kate talked their mom into snow cones from a local stand.

Since Mr. Charlie was coming down later to put up the new fixture, the ceiling needed to be painted that morning. Matthew rolled paint on the ceiling while his mom, using Mr. Charlie's ladder, did the detail work around the edges. Kate sat on the front steps, occasionally being a gofer as Matthew called her. In the past when he was Kate's age, Dad had made Matthew his gofer, sending him for the hammer or a bottle of water—whatever he needed. Now it was Kate's turn.

Matthew had finished rolling the last section when a black

Lexus pulled into the dirt drive. Nice car, thought Matthew. The door of the Lexus opened and a young woman got out. She was dressed in a business suit and her high heels kicked up dust as she walked toward them. She glanced toward the flower bed as she approached the porch.

"Good morning," she said brightly. "I'm looking for Andrea Morin." The woman stopped at the bottom of the brick stairs.

"I am Andrea Morin," said Mom as she climbed down the ladder.

"So nice to meet you. Let me begin by expressing my sympathy for the death of your husband. I cannot even imagine how hard this has been for you."

"Thank you, Ms. . . . what did you say your name was?"

The woman started up the porch stairs, extending her hand toward Matthew's mom. "Heather Jonson. I represent Jonson Land Enterprises."

Mom briefly shook the woman's hand and asked, "And how did you know my name, Ms. Jonson?"

"I had talked to your husband in the past. My company is interested in purchasing land on this side of Caddo Lake, and we're talking to the landowners in this area. I noticed you were here as I passed your house and decided to stop and talk to you in person."

Matthew looked at the road and wondered where she was going. The road dead-ended a little farther down.

"We are not interested in selling any land, Ms. Jonson. I do not have that authority anyway."

"I know that there are other family members on the title, Andrea, and your husband was one of them. You and your children now own his part of the property."

Matthew was beginning to dislike the woman, even though he didn't really know why. "How would you know that?" he asked. He could see his mom's eyes narrowing like they did when she was getting irritated. This pushy woman was standing uninvited on their porch.

"Your name is Matthew, isn't it?" Ms. Jonson asked. "Don't worry, Matt, it's all part of the public record. You know, the papers that are stored at the parish courthouse." She smiled at him.

He glared at the lady who was talking to him as if he were six.

She looked back to Matthew's mom. "Since Jonson Land Enterprises has an interest in the land in this area, we have checked title documents at the courthouse. That way we can talk to landowners directly. With no lawyers involved, we can offer you the most money for the property and file the necessary documents for you."

Matthew stepped forward to stand beside his mom.

"Once again, Ms. Jonson, I cannot sell this land to you. The family is not interested in selling."

"Don't worry about the rest of the family, Andrea. I will be glad to approach the co-owners for their approval. I know how sensitive a matter of selling old family land can be. And please call me Heather. I feel like we already know each other."

"I think my mom wants to you leave, *Heather,*" Matthew said, pronouncing her name sarcastically.

"I hope you will think about it," Heather replied, smiling. Reaching into her large leather handbag, she extended a business card toward Matthew's mom. "I'll check back in a few days. Have a nice afternoon."

Matthew watched her car turn and rattle across the cattle guard onto the road. Instead of turning toward the highway as Matthew expected, she turned to the right, going farther down the road.

"Why did that woman go that way? I thought we were the last house on this road," Matthew said, turning toward his mom.

"Don't know, Matthew." She looked up briefly as the car disappeared beyond the trees.

"Do you think she talked to Uncle Roy?" asked Matthew.

"He didn't mention it last time I talked to him. Okay, kids, let's get this painting mess cleaned up and get some lunch," Mom said. "Kate and I need to bake brownies before Mr. Charlie gets here."

Kate grinned and clapped. "Oh, fun!"

Later that afternoon, Mr. Charlie and his wife, Ms. Sarah, rocked and ate brownies with the family on the porch. The smell of the paint slowly dissipated in the breeze of the new ceiling fan.

"Hey, Mr. Charlie," said Matthew, turning from his perch on the brick steps, "aren't we the last house on this road?"

"You were the last inhabited house, Matt, but someone has been fixin' up that cabin at the end of the road. I've seen his truck go by. He's been workin' on it for a couple of months now, and I've seen smoke comin' from that direction."

"Whatcha think he was burning?" asked Matthew.

"Probably the brush he'd cut down from around the cabin. I haven't met him. Didn't want to intrude, so I haven't gone down there."

"Well, we are glad that you and Sarah 'intrude' here!" Mom said.

Ms. Sarah smiled and, reaching for another brownie, said, "So Kate, I hear that you like to bake. Did you and your mom make these brownies from a mix or from scratch?"

Kate frowned. "What's 'scratch'?" Mom and Ms. Sarah both chuckled. Ms. Sarah went on to explain that 'scratch' referred to measuring and mixing the flour, sugar, cocoa, and other ingredients instead of using a pre-packaged brownie mix. They continued to talk about cooking.

Matthew, who had no interest in the subject of cooking food, just eating it, turned to Mr. Charlie and asked him about Heather. "A lady came by this morning, trying to get us to sell this land. I told her she needed to leave."

"I'm glad you are tryin' to fill your dad's shoes," Mr. Charlie said, smiling and nodding his head. "She's been by my house, too. Pesky lady."

"She told Mom she had already talked to my dad."

"She didn't say what your dad said though, did she? What did your mom say?"

"She told her that we weren't interested and couldn't sell the land anyway. Then that lady said she planned to talk to Uncle Roy—you know, my dad's brother."

"I remember. That's kinda nervy of her comin' up here to talk to your mom like that. Makes me wonder why she wants this land so bad."

"Charlie, we need to go so I can start supper," said Ms. Sarah, standing up from her rocking chair. "Kate, try what I told you about the cornbread. I bet you and your mom can find an old cast iron skillet under the cabinet in the kitchen that will work just fine. See y'all later," she said as she walked down the stairs. Mr. Charlie waved and followed her to the truck.

"All right, kids, about an hour until dinner," Mom said. Cutting her eyes toward them and smiling, she added, "I wonder if that is enough time to go fishing?"

"Kate, want me to show you how to cast into the *lake* instead of into the trees?" Matthew teased.

"I can do it," said Kate. "I'll show you."

Kate rushed into the house to get the fishing gear.

Matthew hesitated a moment and, before following Kate into the house, cast a look at the woods toward the cabin at the end of the road.

Chapter 3

Friday, June 13

On Wednesday and Thursday mornings, Matthew and Kate helped with more work at the farmhouse, dusting and moving furniture to make the sweeping and mopping easier. Mom made Matthew carry the bucket of dirty water to dump it over the fence several times. She insisted. Afternoons gave them time to explore the woods and hang out on the dock. The woods were cooler than the lake, and Matthew liked the fresh scent of the trees and pine straw. The pine trees were widely spaced but one area was even more sparse, forming a small clearing not far into the woods from the house. Kate convinced Matthew to rake pine straw into walls for a pretend log cabin. By Friday morning, free from chores, they were back in the woods. Kate wanted to make her cabin walls seem more realistic and needled Matthew into pulling over some fallen logs to place on the raked pine straw walls.

Being a guest in Kate's pretend cabin was not Matthew's idea of a good time, so he wandered away to explore. Mom had said to keep the house in sight while they were in the woods, but Matthew figured that mainly applied to Kate.

The tall pine trees had dumped plenty of pine straw on the floor of the forest. Not much underbrush grew there. One area, however, had even fewer little saplings or weeds than the others. It seemed to be some kind of trail. Maybe it was a deer path. He could hear Kate behind him inviting imaginary guests into her cabin, so he knew she was fine.

The path beckoned to Matthew. He followed it as it wound through the trees, the cover of the pine trees creating splotchy spots of shadow and sunlight on the trail. He soon lost sight of Kate and her cabin. He was looking down in order to follow the path when it changed direction to go around a sudden slope. He glanced up and realized that he was looking at a small hill, which seemed to rise right out of the ground. The hill curved around slightly and seemed about twice as long as and wider than Mr. Charlie's truck but only about four feet tall. No trees grew on the rise.

The area around the farm was slightly hilly, but the hills were large in diameter and not but a few yards higher than the countryside, what Dad called the rolling hills of north Louisiana. He didn't remember this small hill, but he and Dad didn't usually come this far into the woods on their visits to the farmhouse. They spent their time at the house or around the cleared part of the property, fixing fences or clearing overgrowth.

Climbing the steep hill, he noticed that it was slightly back from the edge of a ridge that dropped down to the shoreline of the lake below. He followed the high part of the rise and cut back down to the path at the other end. He had a good view of the inlet from there. As he turned to walk around the lake side of the rise, he heard Kate calling, "Matt, where are you? Matt . . . ?" Matthew sighed, called out to her, and started walking back her way. The investigation of this hill rising unexpectedly in the woods would have to wait.

"Matt, where'd you go?" Kate asked with furrowed brows as Matthew returned to the clearing.

"It's all right, Kate. I was just down that way, following a trail." He recognized that she had been frightened when she thought she was alone in the woods. He felt a little guilty. What a big difference there was between the ages of almost twelve and seven. "I wasn't far away."

"That's not right, Matt," Kate said, shaking her blonde

head at him. "Mom said to stay close to the house." Matthew thought at any minute she was going to start shaking her finger at him.

"Kate . . . Matthew . . . Lunch." Their mom's voice came through the trees. Heading back to the house, Matthew suddenly realized that he was hungry.

During lunch, Mom told them that they were going back home to Shreveport on Saturday morning. "I want to check the mail and go to church on Sunday. We can pick up some groceries and come back here on Sunday afternoon."

"Hey, Mom, can me and Janie go to the pool on Saturday afternoon?" asked Kate.

Mom smiled at her. "We can do that. Any special request from you, Matthew?"

Matthew frowned as he thought, then he said, "Can Nick and I stay at the house and play video games while y'all go to the pool?"

"I don't really want y'all at the house all alone, Matthew," his mom started to answer.

"But, Mom, I haven't played *Flying Eagles* since last Friday," he started in on his argument. "I have to improve my scores. It's a competition and Nick is getting really good. I need some playing time, and I haven't been able to play—not even once this week!" The words were flying out of his mouth.

"Whoa, whoa," said his mom. She paused and then added, "I know you love playing your video games, but I don't want you home by yourselves. Why don't you and Nick come to the pool with us?"

"Mom, we are almost twelve years old! Why can't we stay at the house by ourselves? It's not like we're going to throw a wild party or anything."

"Bear with me, Matthew. I need you to understand that I can't leave you alone at the house. Not yet."

Matthew glared at his mom and her overprotective attitude. "You have me stranded out here at the farmhouse for a whole week. Then I hear you tell Mr. Charlie that we might stay for two weeks. You didn't even let me bring my video games with me. This is so unfair. Kate likes to play in the woods and chase butterflies, but *I am bored!* I feel like a prisoner out here."

She had been like that since Dad . . . Well, since they've been without his dad. He could hardly think the word "cancer" without a giant lump in his throat.

His mom sighed. After a short silence, she looked up and said, "You're right, Matthew. You are almost twelve. I'll compromise with you. What if Nick comes back with you for the week?" She smiled and added, "And, yes, you can bring the game system. We need to agree on how much time y'all spend playing."

Matthew's shoulders relaxed and the lump in his throat seemed to shrink. "That'll work, Mom. I'm going to call him right now."

"Mom, when do I get to call Janie?" Matthew heard Kate whining as he went to the living room to get Mom's phone. She always left it on top of the piano.

On his way back from the living room after calling Nick, Matthew glanced out the dining room window toward the woods. He saw smoke above the trees. "Hey, Mom, it looks like that man who moved into the old cabin is burning brush again."

"I see it, Matthew," Mom called from the kitchen. After a short pause, she said, "I don't think that smoke is at the cabin. It looks closer—I think it's in our woods! Matthew, call 9-1-1. Kate get the bucket from the pantry."

Matthew heard the screen door slam as he ran back to the living room to get the cellphone. Then he followed Kate out the back door. She was carrying the bucket down the back steps, and Matthew whipped around her as soon as she reached the ground.

"Hey, Mom," Matthew said. He could see her yellow capris as she leaned into the pump house to get the garden hose. "What's the address? I mean, I know how to get here and everything, but I don't know where to tell the firemen to come."

"It's 301 Steward's Inlet Road—the old Morin farmhouse," she said as she dragged the hose across the yard. "Then call Charlie. His number is in my Favorites under Steward." Stretching the hose as far as it would reach, she started spraying the grass and weeds along the fence.

Matthew watched a column of smoke and sparks rise above the trees. He punched in 9-1-1 and told the operator about the fire. Then he found Mr. Charlie's number and punched the call button.

"Our woods are on fire!" Matthew practically yelled into the phone when Mr. Charlie answered.

"Calm down, Matt. Have you called 9-1-1?"

"Yes, sir."

"Which side of the house is the fire on?"

He told him and Mr. Charlie said, "Get the key to the gate in the south fence. The pumper truck will never get through the fence into the yard at the cattle guard. Be right there."

Matthew raced toward the back door; he knew where the keys were kept. His dad had sent him to get them more than once when they were working on their summer projects. He grabbed the gate keys from the nail in the pantry and rushed back out the door as Mr. Charlie's truck pulled into the drive. Matthew thought he could hear the siren of the fire truck in the distance.

"Matt, you got the key? Run down to open that gate," Mr. Charlie said as he and Ms. Sarah got out of their truck. "Andrea, you might want to spray the roof."

Matthew picked his way across the pipes in the cattle guard past the barbed wire and then ran down the fence by the big oak tree to the south gate. Mr. Charlie was not far behind him. He and Mr. Charlie opened the long metal galvanized gate, pushing it over some high weeds. On his way back, he noticed Kate standing in the middle of the side yard with tears streaming down her cheeks. She held up the bucket to show Ms. Sarah. As he reentered the yard, Matthew heard Ms. Sarah say, "Kate, we can fill up that bucket and then you can pour it on the grass by the fence. Matt, where is there another spigot?"

"On the far side of the porch," Matthew said, pointing to the right of the house.

Ms. Sarah led Kate that way as Mom sprayed water on the roof. A red pickup truck with "911" painted on the side and a pumper truck turned into the south fence gate where Mr. Charlie stood directing them. He then walked back to the yard.

"What happened, Matt?" he asked.

"I don't know, Mr. Charlie. I just noticed the fire in the woods after lunch."

Mr. Charlie stared in the direction of the fire as Kate poured her bucket of water along the fence line. Kate trotted back to Ms. Sarah to get more water.

Within a few minutes a man in a dark blue shirt with a fire captain patch on the front joined them in the yard and announced, "Fire's out." Mr. Charlie turned off the water hose at the pump house and then introduced Matthew's mom to Chief Mitch Williams. The chief looked at Matthew and Kate and asked, "Have you kids been playing in the woods?"

Both Matthew and Kate nodded their heads.

"Did you rake up the pine straw?"

"Only some of it into some kind of walls to make a cabin for Kate to play in," Matthew said, feeling a little nervous from the chief's serious look.

"Did you move some fallen logs?"

"I moved some logs this morning so Kate could have log walls for her make-believe cabin."

"Why do you ask, Chief?" asked Mom. "Is that what was on fire?"

"Well, ma'am, the logs were pushed to the center of

a cleared area of ground. That's what was burning. The fire had not spread yet because the pine straw had been raked away from the logs. Is this rake yours?" He held up a yard rake.

"I guess I left it in the woods," Kate said. Her lower lip started to quiver and tears rolled down her cheeks again. Ms. Sarah put her arm around Kate's shoulders and Kate leaned toward her.

"But we didn't rake the pine straw *away*, and we didn't put the logs in a pile. I told you, I put the logs in a square as walls for her cabin!" Matthew said. He felt like the chief was trying to blame them for the fire.

Chief Williams glanced back at the woods with a worried look on his face as a deputy sheriff's car pulled into the drive. Inside the south fence gate, a couple of firemen were putting the hoses back on the truck.

"Hey, Doug," the chief said as the deputy got out of his car. "You're a little late for this party. Didn't take us long to put out that bonfire."

"Yeah, I was north of town when I heard the call," the deputy said. "What caused it?"

"That's the mystery. Kids say they were playing in the woods earlier, but what they describe and what I found don't match up."

Mom looked at the chief with raised brow and widened eyes. "Are you suggesting that my children are lying?"

"We didn't have matches or anything. I know better than that!" Matthew said.

The deputy looked with slightly raised eyebrows at the chief and seemed to be waiting for the answer himself. "Well, I have told you what I found," the chief said. "The fire appears to be deliberately set. I don't know who set it or why. It's out now, and I don't think you'll have any more problems." He turned to walk across the cattle guard to his waiting truck.

Mr. Charlie called after him, "Thanks, Mitch."

"Yes, thank you," said Mom.

Chief Williams waved his hand in acknowledgment and the trucks soon left.

"Andrea, this is Doug Ramsey. Doug, Andrea Morin," Mr. Charlie said as Mom and the deputy shook hands.

"You want a cup of coffee, Doug? Won't take a minute to make," said Ms. Sarah. "Come on, Andrea. You and the children come on up to the house for a while. Hey, Kate, you still have any of those brownies?"

"Yes, ma'am," nodded Kate, smiling. "Mom and I made a bunch." She ran into the house.

Within a few minutes the group gathered on the Stewards' back porch under the fan discussing the situation. Holding a steaming cup of coffee, Deputy Ramsey asked, "So what can you tell me about this fire? When did it start?"

"Matthew noticed the smoke after lunch, probably about one o'clock," answered Mom.

"You kids were playing in the woods?"

"We were in the woods this morning, but we didn't start the fire," Matthew said, his voice displaying the insulting attitude he was feeling. Matthew was getting tired of being accused of causing the fire.

"No, son, I'm not saying that," said the deputy patiently. "I only want to get my facts straight."

"It's all right, Matt," said Mr. Charlie. "Just answer his questions with what you know. Deputy Ramsey is not saying you did anything wrong."

Matthew looked at Mr. Charlie and nodded his head. Then he turned to the deputy. "Well, sir, like I told the fire chief, Kate wanted a pretend cabin with pine straw to indicate where the walls are. That's why the rake was in the woods. But then she wanted real walls. So I pulled some fallen logs into a square for her. That's all we did. I swear." Kate nodded her head in agreement. She snuggled beside Mom, who patted her leg.

"Doug, Mitch said that the logs had been piled up and

the area around that had been raked clear. Looks like someone was in those woods after the children left."

"Mr. Charlie," Matthew said quietly, "what about that man you said moved into the cabin at the end of the road?"

"Not Herbert Washington," said the deputy. "He wouldn't have set a fire in the woods."

"But Mr. Charlie said he saw smoke coming from that way after the man moved in," said Matthew.

"Mr. Washington is a retired Wildlife and Fisheries agent. And, by the way, a direct descendant of the Caddo Indians. He has a lot of respect for the woods and the damage that a fire could do."

Matthew sat on the steps with his elbows on his knees and his chin propped in his hands, listening to the adults rehash the fire. This situation was weird. Someone had moved the logs that he used to make Kate's cabin. Someone had raked the pine straw away from the logs. He guessed they did that so the fire wouldn't spread. That was strange. Why start a fire and then keep it from spreading?

Then it struck him—*someone* had been in *their* woods. And so close to the house. Matthew thought about how he had left Kate by herself! What would Dad have said about that? No matter what the others believed, Matthew knew he had to keep watch for the man from the cabin.

Chapter 4

Monday, June 16

Matthew, his family, and his friend, Nick, got back to the farmhouse late Sunday night. Sitting on the dock after breakfast on Monday morning, the boys finally had an opportunity to talk by themselves. Matthew had plenty to tell Nick about the fire as they cast their fishing lines into the lake.

"So, Matt, you saying that someone set that fire on purpose?" Nick wiggled his slightly pudgy toes in the water. He kicked water toward a turtle resting on a log at the shoreline.

"It looks that way."

"Have you seen where the fire was since then?"

"Nope."

Nick turned to look straight at Matthew, smiling. "Let's go look at it."

"I don't know, Nick. Maybe we shouldn't go in the woods." Matthew looked down at the expanding ripple where the turtle slid into the water.

"You scared?" Nick teased.

"No. I thought about going. I think I need to know why someone set a fire in our woods."

Getting up and reeling in his line, Nick said confidently, "Exactly what I want to find out. Let's go. We need to have a look at the crime scene." He slipped his bare feet into his Crocs.

Matthew reeled in his line slowly, not sure about going into the woods. He tried one more time to divert Nick's attention. "What about playing *Flying Eagles?*"

"Oh, come on, Matt. This is more exciting. This is real life," said Nick as he walked down the dock.

"That's what worries me," Matthew grumbled to himself. He put on his sneakers and got to his feet. Picking up the fishing gear, he followed Nick.

When they reached the end of the dock, they heard Mom calling to them from up the hill. Nick looked at Matthew and asked, "Do you know what she wants?"

"Nope," Matthew answered.

Looking over Nick's shoulder, he saw his mom and a strange girl standing at the top of the hill. Her long, brown hair was shining in the morning sun. She looked about their age. Matthew and Nick put down the gear at the end of the dock and walked up the hill.

"Boys, this is Abigail," Mom said as they approached. "She's Charlie and Sarah's granddaughter."

Matthew looked at Abigail. She was dressed in a T-shirt and shorts and held a really thick book at her side.

"She arrived Saturday and will be visiting them all this week. Charlie thought she might enjoy some company her own age." Pointing to each boy as she spoke, she added, "Abigail, this is Matthew and Nick."

"Hey," both Matthew and Nick mumbled.

"Hey," she muttered back.

"Well, I'll leave y'all to get acquainted. Why don't you go back to fishing? Are you catching anything?"

"Just hard luck," Nick said under his breath. Matthew had to bite his lip to keep from laughing. They walked back to the dock, picking up their gear as they went. Abigail followed.

Matthew and Nick returned to casting their fishing lines. Abigail sat cross-legged a little ways from them and opened her book. After ten minutes of quiet, Nick looked at Matthew and said, "This sucks."

"What does?" Abigail looked up from her book.

"Being stuck on this dock with you," said Nick. "We had better things to do, and then you showed up."

"Nick! You don't have to be rude. It's not her fault." Matthew was a little embarrassed by the blunt comment.

"I did see you reeling in your lines when I came out the back door," said Abigail. She didn't seem upset or insulted like a lot of girls would have been. "What were you going to do?"

"You wouldn't be interested," came the sarcastic comment from Nick. "You probably couldn't crawl far enough out of that book to get involved in our adventure. That book must weigh a ton!"

"When Granddad told me that I was going to visit two boys, I figured I was in for a marathon video game session. I brought a book so that I could at least have something to do while you two were completely absorbed in shooting aliens or crashing cars." She wound her long hair up into a knot and secured it on the back of her head with one of those covered rubber bands like Mom used in Kate's hair. "I'm ready for something to do. I've read this book twice before." She held up her copy of *Harry Potter and the Goblet of Fire.*

"I've read that book," said Matthew. "It's good. Did you read *Hunger Games?*"

"Yeah and *Catching Fire,* too. I haven't seen the movies yet though. Except for Harry Potter, I don't think the movies are ever as good as the books."

"You got that right," said Matthew. "Have you read . . ."

"Hey, you two," interrupted Nick, "this is not a book report. *Yuck.* Makes me think of the summer reading list." He looked at Abby. "If you must know, we were about to investigate that fire site. But anyone who comes to a dock with a book that big probably isn't into adventure."

"Oh, the mysterious fire!" Abigail placed her closed book on the dock and leaned forward. "I heard my parents talking to my grandparents about that. It sounds so intriguing. I love mysteries. I was hoping to get a look at the place where it happened."

"Well, Abigail, Matt and I were planning to solve that *mysterious fire* before you showed up."

Abby rose to her feet and put her hands on her hips. "I'll have you know, Nick, I'm probably better at solving mysteries than both of you put together." Her sarcasm practically melted the boards under her feet. "Let's go." She put her book at the end of the dock and started up the hill. "And call me Abby!" she yelled down to them.

The boys hurriedly stashed the fishing gear at the bottom of the hill in order to keep up with her.

"You have to admit, she doesn't climb this hill like a bookworm," said Matthew. Nick only grunted.

At the top of the hill, Abby turned toward them and asked, "Which way?"

"South of the house," Matthew answered as he pointed. Dad had always used directions rather than left or right when referring to areas around the house, explaining that directions worked, no matter which way a person was standing. He cast a quick glance at the house to make sure Mom wasn't looking their way. He figured it was better if she didn't know they were going to look at the fire's location.

At the fence Matthew pulled apart two of the wires of the barbed-wire fence as Abby and Nick took turns climbing through, being careful not to get caught on the barbs. Then Nick did the same for him.

Matthew had led them only a little way into the woods when they spotted the pile of burned logs centered in the dirt clearing. The acrid smell of the burned pine logs was strong.

"Wow. This is close to the house," Abby said, glancing back. She walked around the edge on the pine straw, looking at the scene. The boys followed her.

"Now, Matt, tell us everything that happened," Abby said as she settled onto a pile of the pine straw. She pulled up her bare legs and put her arms around her bent knees.

Matthew and Nick sat down as well. Nick picked a piece of pine straw out of his Crocs.

Matthew described the cabin-building episode, the pine straw walls, and the addition of the fallen-log walls. He also told them about going back to the house for lunch.

"Then I went to call Nick on Mom's cell phone. On my way back, I saw the smoke out the dining room window. I don't remember seeing the fire itself. I'm surprised I didn't, as well as we can see the house from here." He looked toward the house.

"Did you notice anyone in the woods while you were here that morning?" Abby asked. "Maybe a movement or something out of the corner of your eye?"

Matthew shook his head and looked down at the ground. He grabbed a stick and started drawing in a spot of dirt illuminated by a small shaft of sunlight.

"There's something you aren't telling us, isn't there?" Nick said, tipping his head to the side as he watched his friend.

Matthew tried to look unconcerned. He didn't want to admit that he had left Kate by herself, especially in front of Nick. And he had just met Abby. What would she think?

"Tell us, Matt," said Abby. "Any little detail could be important."

"I don't know if anyone else was close to this area of the woods because I left," he said quietly. "I started following a trail that led that way." He pointed the stick to the southwest, away from the house and closer to the lake.

"How far did you go?" asked Nick.

"I don't know. I found a hill and was climbing it. I wasn't thinking about Kate." Matthew looked down at his feet again. "I feel so bad. I shouldn't have left her alone. Whoever set that fire could have gotten her."

Nick was silent. Abby looked at Matthew and said, "Okay, let's consider the facts, Matt." She stood up and walked around. "Look at this cleared area. The pile of pine straw is at least five feet away from the burned logs. Whoever set this fire was obviously not trying to hurt anyone."

"And," said Nick, "we can see the house from here." He

leaned to the left in order to see between the trees toward the house. "They must have known you would see the fire before it got out of hand."

"I agree," said Abby. "I don't think they wanted to harm anyone."

Matthew looked up at them with a slight smile. He knew they were trying to make him feel better, and he appreciated it. "I haven't told anyone else about leaving Kate."

"We'll keep your secret. Right, Abby?" said Nick as he looked at Abby who nodded in agreement.

After a brief pause, she said, "So we know someone was here. We still need to find evidence of where the person or persons came from. Let's check around the area. Maybe we can see where the person walked." She scouted the area between the fire and the trees beside the road. The boys looked around the far side of the burned area.

"Look, the pine straw is all scuffed up here."

The boys rushed over to where Abby pointed.

"It sure is," said Nick.

Matthew frowned, disappointed. "That is probably where the firemen walked. They drove their truck as close as they could get and then dragged their hoses in."

"Well, of course," said Abby. "The firemen."

Nick looked through the trees toward the road, surveying the area. "What did they hook the hose to? There's not a fire hydrant around here."

"They used a pumper truck. If I hadn't been so rattled while they were here, it would have been cool to watch how it all worked," said Matthew. "It was all over pretty fast. I guess they had enough water in the tank. They had the fire out in no time."

"Just think; whoever set the fire could have been watching it be put out. Maybe it's an arsonist who likes to watch his work. He could have been standing over there." Nick pointed toward the lake, looking pleased with himself.

"I hope not, Nick," said Matthew. "He might have my house in mind for his next fire."

"But," said Abby thoughtfully, "maybe Nick has the right idea about where the arsonist was coming from. Maybe he came from the lake side."

"He would have had to get here by boat," said Matthew.

"Or through the woods that way," said Nick, pointing farther south away from the house.

"There is a man who lives in a cabin on the other side of these woods," said Matthew. "Mr. Charlie said he has seen smoke coming from that direction."

"So, he's into fire," said Nick.

"Let's look over there," said Abby, pointing toward the woods on the lake side.

They skirted the area of the burned logs and began searching the other side of the clearing.

"Here's a path," said Nick.

"That's the one I followed on Friday," said Matthew.

"That's probably not the way someone came then," said Abby. "You would have seen someone on your way back."

"That's one thing that bothers me," said Matthew, stopping to look at the other two. "The timing. Kate and I went right back to the house and ate lunch when Mom called. Yet this person had put the logs into a pile and set them on fire by the time we finished our sandwiches. Doesn't that seem kind of fast?"

"You said that you had already pulled the logs into the area for Kate," said Abby.

"Yeah. They were in a square right there." Matthew pointed to the burned logs.

"Well, all someone had to do was pull them together and set them on fire," said Nick.

"And rake the pine straw away from the logs. I guess they used a branch or brought a rake with them," said Abby.

"We left our rake in the woods," Matthew said.

"Well, that was nice of you. I guess the arsonist appreciated that!" Nick said drily.

"Can we quit calling this guy the arsonist?" said Matthew exasperated. "We don't know that someone did this on purpose."

"I'm sorry, Matt. I know you don't want to believe that someone is hanging around your woods, but that is the way it looks," said Abby. "This guy had at the most maybe thirty minutes to rake pine straw, pull logs into a pile, and set the fire before you noticed. I think that's long enough, but I'm guessing that person had to have been close by."

Matthew frowned. He kind of shivered. *Creepy.* He felt a responsibility to protect his mom and sister—his dad's girls. He had to try to do what his dad would have done. But what *would* his dad have done?

About that time, something toward the house caught his eye.

The hawk.

It flew over the house and went toward the lake.

"You know what, guys, we better make our way back to the dock. Let's go toward the lake and look that way. Then we can cut back to the dock," he said.

"The best way to avoid your mother, Matt?" asked Nick with a smile as they wound their way between trees.

"I don't want to worry her," he said. "This is our little conspiracy, okay, guys?"

Abby and Nick both nodded.

They cut back under the fence close to the lake and were crossing the yard by the water when they heard Matthew's mom calling them. The boys grabbed the fishing gear, Abby grabbed her book, and they all climbed the hill to the house.

"Abigail, want to have lunch with us?" Kate called from the back door.

"Sure," said Abby. As she got to the steps, she added, "And Kate, call be Abby."

Matthew noticed Abby chatting with Kate during lunch. He thought it was nice of her to be kind to his little sister.

As Mom was asking Abby if she wanted to help her and Kate bake cookies, Ms. Sarah showed up to take her granddaughter grocery shopping with her.

Abby lagged a little behind her grandma and Matthew's mom as they walked down the front steps toward Ms. Sarah's car. "Keep thinking about that day," she said. "There's got to be other clues. I'll try to come back tomorrow."

Matthew and Nick nodded.

After Ms. Sarah's car pulled onto the road, Nick turned to Matthew, "Okay, Matt, now it's time to 'shoot down aliens and crash cars' as Abby so eloquently put our video game playing."

"She was okay, though," said Matthew, heading with Nick into the dining room to play.

"She seemed to be really interested in the fire."

"Yeah," said Matthew, giving a nervous glance towards the woods.

CHAPTER 5

TUESDAY, JUNE 17

The next morning, while Matthew and Nick were lingering at the breakfast table, Mom took her coffee cup to the front porch. Then Matthew heard his Mom call good morning to Abby. "Matthew . . . Nick . . . Abby's here."

Abby returned her greeting as Nick and Matthew walked out the living room door.

Nick looked around and asked, "Did you walk all the way down here?"

"It's only about a quarter of a mile," Matthew said.

"Hey," said Kate, coming out the front door still eating her biscuit. "Want to see my room?"

"Okay. For a minute." Abby disappeared into the house.

"Kate, finish that biscuit in the dining room," called Mom.

The boys sat down on the porch steps. Matthew had not been able to come up with a good reason for going back into the woods. He hoped that Abby had a plan. She reappeared on the porch. "Nice dollhouse," she said.

"Her dad made it last summer," Matthew replied. "We added some furniture at Christmas. She loves it."

"I can see why." Abby paused. "Mrs. Morin, Granddad said that this area used to be a community for the Caddo Indians. I was wondering if Matt and Nick and I could walk around by the lake and in the woods looking for arrowheads."

Matthew and Nick glanced at each other. Matthew smiled, thinking it was a good plan.

"Yeah, Mom, that sounds like fun," Matthew said. "You didn't want us to spend all of our time playing video games. This gets us out of the house."

He saw his mom's hesitant look. When was she going to stop treating him like a child? If Dad were here . . . But then she sighed and said, "I guess that would be all right if you keep the house within sight and stay away from that burn site. I don't want you wandering around in those woods." Then she added, "And grab water bottles from the refrigerator to take with you. It's really hot and humid this morning."

As Matthew, Abby, and Nick walked to the kitchen to get the water, Abby said, "I think we should begin where we left off yesterday."

"That's what I was thinking," said Matthew, "and now we don't have to sneak to do it. Good idea, Abby."

Abby smiled. "Actually, my granddad really was telling me about the Caddo Indian community here. That's when I got the idea."

They went down the back steps and headed into the side yard. As they climbed through the barbed-wire fence, Matthew glanced back at the house. His mom, still holding her coffee cup, was watching from the porch. She turned and went into the house.

"Let's stay close to the fence line for a few minutes," Matthew told the others.

"So your mom won't get worried?" asked Nick.

Matthew nodded.

In no time, the three were standing at the burn site.

"So, Matt, you didn't see any strange cars on your road on Friday?" asked Abby.

"No. Nobody much comes down our road," said Matthew. "Here's the trail I took." Both Abby and Nick looked that way, but the morning shadows were deep, making it hard to see down the trail.

"Well, let's go," said Nick.

"Maybe the person who set the fire left this way," said Abby.

They wound their way along the narrow trail for a couple

of minutes. The only things they saw were squirrels and pine cones. The trail soon angled around the rise. "This is the small hill that I found," Matthew said. They climbed up the rise and looked toward the lake.

"Why does this part of the woods seem different somehow?" asked Abby, looking around at the trees nearby.

"I noticed that too," said Nick. "But I don't see anything different. Although something seems familiar about this hill."

Matthew looked down the fifteen-foot ridge between the rise and the lake. "Someone could have climbed up this ridge from the lake."

All three walked down the hill and along the top edge of the ridge.

"This little hill seems to be set back some from the ridge," said Abby. She took a few steps away and looked back. "Almost like the dirt was put here."

"Why would someone pile dirt here?" asked Nick.

"Maybe someone dug a pond or something like that," said Abby. "But the dirt wouldn't be here. The pond in Granddad's pasture has the dirt all piled at the low end, kind of like a dam."

"Was there once a pond here?" asked Nick.

"Don't think so. This was a pasture," Matthew said. "Dad always told me that they used the lake to water the cattle. He didn't mention any ponds. And doesn't a pond need a creek or something for a water source? The creek is on the other side of the house."

"Maybe it was a pond, but they filled it back in," said Nick.

"Maybe." Abby cocked her head to one side as if considering the idea. "But wouldn't they have used this dirt to refill the pond?"

Matthew walked around to the other side of the rise, looking at the area back toward the road. "The ground doesn't seem to sink in like there used to be a hole here.

But there's so many trees, it's hard to tell."

They strolled around to the east side of the rise, the side away from the lake, looking at the ground.

The woods rustled to the south of where the three were standing. Abby leaned forward between the two boys. "Hey, guys, someone or something is over there, to the right," she quietly told them. They turned to look, but only caught a glimpse of a brown movement in the trees.

"I wonder if the fire guy came back?" said Matthew.

"Let's fan out and see if we can find him," said Nick.

Matthew stared at him. "Nick, what exactly would we do if we found him?"

"Okay, then, grab a stick," said Nick, looking around on the ground. "Find a good strong one."

"Maybe we should get better prepared to chase someone before we try that."

"Right now we should get out of the woods and go down by the lake," said Abby.

"This is not a game, Nick. You have to get more serious," said Matthew. "Remember someone set the fire."

"Y'all are no fun," grumbled Nick.

Matthew, Abby, and Nick scrambled their way down the ridge to the narrow flat shore of the lake. They looked back up at the rise and the woods around it. "I am sure someone was there," said Abby.

Matthew thought of his new neighbor. He told Nick and Abby what the deputy had said about the man. "He's a Caddo Indian," Matthew added. "The deputy told me that. Your granddad says he sticks to himself. He hasn't met him."

"Wow. A real Indian?" asked Nick.

"Really, Nick?" Abby rolled her eyes at Nick in annoyance.

"I'll bet he knows how to move through the woods quietly and without anyone seeing where he's been," said Nick.

"I think you may have watched too many old Westerns," said Matthew, smiling at Nick.

"How far to his cabin?" asked Nick. "He could have been the one that set the fire."

"About as far south from our house as Mr. Charlie's house is north."

"Why set a fire on your land? He has his own land right here by the lake, too," said Abby. "But since he is so close by, we could check out his cabin."

Matthew frowned but nodded his head.

"I wonder if he knows that this area was once an Indian community?" asked Nick.

"It would help if we knew more about the Caddo Indians," said Abby. "Maybe it's time for some background research."

"I knew it was too good to last," said Nick. "She is reverting back to her bookworm self."

"We need more information," Abby said matter-of-factly, starting to walk toward the dock. "Matt, do you have internet at your house?"

"Only on my mom's phone."

"Then let's go to my grandparents' house. We'll use their computer."

"Your grandparents have a computer?" asked Matthew, a little surprised.

"Of course. My grandma used a computer on her job before she retired."

"What'd she do?" asked Nick.

"She was the secretary at the high school. Now she uses it for email and Facebook, keeping in touch with family and friends and stuff. And she likes genealogy. She looks up information on our family." She stopped and turned toward the boys with a bright look in her eyes. "In fact, she told me to be back by ten o'clock since she is going to the library to do some research. We could go with her and look up info there."

"I liked the internet idea better," said Nick. "We could just Google it."

"What would we tell my mom?" said Matthew. "She

won't buy a story about me and Nick wanting to go to the library to do research."

"What if we tell her we're going to check out the summer reading books?" asked Nick. "We could say that Abby has already read two of them and she said she would help us."

"She might buy that from you, Nick, as much as you *love* to read," said Matthew in a dry tone. Then he added seriously, "However, she would tell me that I need to read the books myself."

"Then make this only about me. I don't like to read. Abby is here. I need help. Will she buy that?"

"I'm game," said Abby. "We need to know more. Where did the Indians live in this area? How can we tell where they lived? What do we look for?"

Matthew nodded. "Let's head to the house. We have to see if Mom will let us go." The three reached the dock area and turned to trudge up the hill toward the house.

"I know she will since Grandma is taking us," said Abby.

Ten minutes later, Abby and the two boys were in the SUV with Kate and Mom going to the Steward house. They had already called Abby's grandmother and gotten permission to go with her.

"Have you got some money, Matthew?" Mom asked as they climbed out of the SUV. "Y'all might go to Dairy Queen or something."

"Yes, ma'am. I have twenty dollars."

"But, Mommy, I want to go to the library too. Why can't I go?" said Kate.

"You already have some library books, Kate. You and I can go to Walmart and pick up some ice cream. How does that sound?" his mom said.

"Can I buy something for my dollhouse?"

"We'll see. Okay, Matthew, call me when you get back so I can pick you up," she said as Matthew, Abby, and Nick jumped out of the SUV in the Steward's driveway.

During the trip into town in Ms. Sarah's car, Abby and the

boys talked only about summer reading books. Matthew could check out books since this library was a branch of the larger one he used in Shreveport.

They waited until they were in the special Louisiana section of the library to talk about their real purpose for coming.

They located the correct shelf and found several books on the Caddo Indians. "We can each grab a book and look through it for info and then share what we find with each other," said Abby. Looking pointedly at Nick, she added, "Yes, Nick, you will have to *read*."

"I can read—especially when I want to." Nick grabbed a book and sat down at a nearby table. Matthew and Abby smiled at Nick's reaction. Then they selected books and joined Nick at the table.

After several minutes of flipping pages and reading titles and captions, Matthew said, "This is a lot of info."

"There are lots of words, lots of words . . ." muttered Nick, as he flipped pages. "Oh, look, here's a picture." He turned the book for the others to see.

"Oh, a map of where the Caddo Indians lived," said Abby. "They definitely lived around here."

"Our house and your grandparents' house are in the middle of the marked area."

"It looks like they may even have lived as far west as where I live."

"Exactly where do you live, Abby?" asked Matthew.

"In Tyler."

"Texas?" asked Nick.

"Yes, Nick. Tyler, Texas."

They continued flipping through the books. After a few more minutes, Abby added, "Did y'all know that there were several Indian groups, and each group had its own name? 'Caddo' was a term that was short for 'Kadohadacho,' one of those groups. It seems the European explorers referred to all of them as 'Caddo' in their records."

"That's great and all, Abby, but how does that help us now?" asked Nick.

"I just thought it was interesting," she muttered.

"I haven't seen anything that tells how to find an old town site," said Matthew.

About that time, Abby's grandmother appeared from behind one of the stacks. Matthew noticed that her clothes were a little dressier than Mr. Charlie's usual jeans and casual button-up shirts. Knowing that she had worked at the high school seemed to explain that.

"I was looking for y'all," Ms. Sarah said. "Did you find the books you wanted?"

"Some of them, Grandma. Can we have a few more minutes?"

"Okay, Abby, ten minutes. But then we have to go." Her grandmother walked toward the checkout desk.

"Guys, we need to check out these books and get that novel Nick is supposed to be reading."

"Abby, won't it look suspicious if I check out all these books?" Matthew said.

Abby leaned around the stacks to look at her grandmother standing at the checkout desk talking to the librarian. "I don't see my grandma holding any books. She can check out these, and then you can get the novel."

"How are you going to explain why you want these books?" asked Nick.

"Don't you remember that my granddad was telling me about the Caddo Indians? My grandma will not think anything is strange about me checking out these books. I often read books about subjects I'm interested in."

Nick rolled his eyes. "Uh oh, your bookworm is showing!" he teased Abby.

The three quickly located the novel on the summer reading list and approached the check-out counter.

When the librarian saw the Caddo Indian books they were checking out, she said, "Did y'all notice the flyer about the lecture tonight?" She pointed to the flyer taped to the counter entitled "The Indians of Caddo: The Early Settlers of Northwest Louisiana."

"Oh, the speaker is Bill Jones," said Ms. Sarah. "He wrote that book about the Caddo Indians. Abby, do you want to go?"

Abby and Matthew exchanged a knowing look. "I think we might want to go, Grandma," Abby said.

"A lecture?" moaned Nick.

"Well, it's not so much of a lecture as a talk with visuals," said the librarian. "I have seen Bill talk before. He is very animated and entertaining."

Matthew looked pointedly at Nick. "Yeah, that would be great," said Nick although his tone was slightly flat.

The group had hamburgers and fries at the Dairy Queen before going back to the house. Rain started to fall on the way back.

"Oh no," said Abby.

"Well, looks like our 'arrowhead hunting' is over for today," said Nick quietly, looking at the flash of lightning above the woods.

"Why don't you both stay with Abby at our house this afternoon?" said Ms. Sarah. "The back porch is nice during a rainfall. You can read your books."

Matthew looked at Nick, who nodded. "Sounds good to us. May I call my mom when we get to your house?"

The three spent the afternoon drinking lemonade and flipping through the books on the Caddo Indians. Nick found information about deer and buffalo hunts, which he thought were awesome. Matthew found information about the Great Log Raft that had once blocked several miles of the Red River, causing smaller waterways to back up.

"But wouldn't that have caused the lake level to be

higher than it is now?" he wondered aloud. "I had begun to think that the town was down the ridge and closer to the lake, but this seems to make that impossible."

"Unless they settled there before the water was higher," said Nick.

"Or the town was closer to where your house is now," said Abby.

"I wonder how long the river was blocked?" said Matthew.

"Maybe we can find something more about it on the internet," said Abby. The group moved inside to the den where the computer was located.

After ten minutes of looking, the three learned that the Great Log Raft had been made from fallen trees and debris that had blocked the river until the mid-1800s. It had even caused small lakes to form like one called Silver Lake in downtown Shreveport that disappeared when the debris was removed.

"Maybe the Indians moved away from the lake when it began to rise," said Matthew.

"Yeah," said Nick. "That's why we can't find anything."

"But we really don't know what we are looking for," said Abby.

"Hey, kids, do y'all want a snack?" Ms. Sarah called from the kitchen.

"Be right there, Grandma. Okay, guys, maybe tonight at the library we can hear something that will help us figure out what to look for."

"Great," grumbled Nick, "I have to go to class when I'm not even in school."

Ignoring Nick's complaining, Matthew said, "If it stops raining tomorrow, let's go back to the woods."

Nick and Abby nodded in agreement.

In the meeting room of the library that night, Mr. Jones

did turn out to be an entertaining speaker, keeping the interest of the audience, even Nick, with his stories, maps, and illustrations. The drawings of the towns showed round, thatched-roof houses, not teepees like Matthew expected. Mr. Jones also had actual artifacts from town sites: arrowheads, fragments of a pottery vessel, and mussel shells.

He stated that finding these items could be an indication of the location of a town.

Someone in the audience asked him about the mussel shells, since Caddo Parish was not adjacent to a salt-water area. Mr. Jones explained that these were fresh-water mussels that had been abundant in Caddo Lake in years past. The Caddo Indians used mussels for food and the shells for decorations.

"These shells, especially the painted ones, and other artifacts can be of high value today," Mr. Jones told the audience. "I know of one man who sold a stone ax head a few weeks ago for more than $400."

Mr. Jones said that another indicator of town sites was the presence of mounds. He showed pictures of the mound discovered several years earlier near the Red River close to the town of Belcher. That was only about fifteen miles from Vivian.

Matthew leaned toward Nick and Abby. "I wish we could go there."

Ms. Sarah looked at him with her finger on her lips.

"These sites are rare and actively sought after," Mr. Jones continued. "The Caddo Nation controls when and who digs on sites; however, scavengers have been known to dig them up to find artifacts to sell."

"That's illegal," said Nick.

"That's right," said Mr. Jones, "but they do it anyway. There are plenty of gold diggers and unscrupulous people in this world. The Caddo Nation and local law enforcement try to keep a close watch on that illegal enterprise."

He ended his talk with the names of books, including his,

and a list of good websites for more information.

When the group stood up to leave, Matthew noticed an older man with long black hair standing against the wall in the back of the room. The man nodded his head at Matthew and then slipped out the back door.

Matthew turned to Nick and Abby. "Did you see that man leaning against the wall in the back?" They both looked, but the man was already gone.

"Who was it?" asked Nick.

"I don't know, but he seemed to know me."

Later that night, the lights were already out in the back corner bedroom the boys were sharing when suddenly Nick said, "Matt!"

"Huh?" Matthew was almost asleep.

"Hey, wake up."

"What is it?" He propped on his elbow and looked out the window into the dark night toward the carport. "Is someone outside?" It was hard to see outside. The only light was on a pole in the front corner of the yard.

Nick sat up in his bed. "No. That's not it. Do you remember the social studies project I did last year?"

"I remember how much you griped about it," said Matthew, sitting up.

"Yeah, well, I guess I did, but I must have actually learned something."

"Do we have to talk about this now? Go to sleep." Matthew turned to fluff his pillow.

"No, Matt, listen," said Nick, turning to face Matthew, sitting up and putting his feet on the floor between the two beds. "Don't you remember the display I made? It was an Indian mound."

"Oh, right. You made it out of clay and covered it with model grass."

"My dad was so impressed that I was interested in something for school that he took me to see a real Indian mound. I wish now that you had gone with us."

"Yeah. Now can we go to sleep?" Matthew lay back down.

Nick rose out of his bed and walked over to Matthew's. "Dad took me to Poverty Point. If you had gone, you would see why I am so excited now."

"Okay, clue me in," Matthew said as he again sat up in the bed.

"That's why that hill in the woods seemed so familiar to me. I think that dirt pile is an Indian mound!"

Chapter 6

Wednesday morning, June 18

The next morning the sky was bright blue and clear after the rain the afternoon before. Matthew and Nick were already on the porch when Abby walked up. The three went inside to talk to Matthew's mom about letting them go back into the woods, but Matthew could tell his mom was still apprehensive about it.

"Last night Mr. Jones said that rain often uncovers hidden pieces," Matthew said. "Yesterday's rain could have uncovered arrowheads that are just under the dirt. This is the perfect time to look."

"I can't ignore the fact that someone set the woods on fire, Matthew. I don't feel right about y'all being in those woods."

"Okay, Mrs. M, we'll play video games," said Nick. Abby and Matthew turned to stare at him. When he winked at them, Matthew hoped Nick had a plan.

"Come on, Abby. The TV is set up in the dining room," said Matthew.

Within a few minutes, all three of them were playing a car crash game with the volume turned up loud.

"Matthew, can y'all turn that down?" his mom said.

"Sure," he said and adjusted the sound. But they didn't turn down the volume on their reactions to the action.

Abby hollered, "You missed that turn, Nick. Go left!"

"Hold on, I've got to get back on the track!"

"Oh, splash! I'm in the water hazard!" groaned Matthew.

"Quit running into me!"

"Then stay out of my way!"

After about ten minutes, Mom came up behind the group with her hands on her hips. "I think y'all need to go out on the porch or down to the dock."

"Okay." Matthew reached over to turn off the video game and then turned to look up at her. "Can we go into the edge of the woods? Please, Mom. We'll be careful."

Nick and Abby also looked up at her, waiting.

Mom looked at the three and sighed. "Make sure that you stay within hollering distance."

"Let's go," said Abby, hopping up from the floor.

"Wait. Got to get something," said Matthew as he headed down the hallway. He was back in a flash, carrying a backpack.

"Y'all stay together," said Mom. "If you see or hear anything strange, you come out of those woods immediately."

Matthew, Abby, and Nick nodded, hurried down the steps, and headed across the yard toward the woods.

"I'm surprised that Kate hasn't begged to go with us," said Nick. "My warty little sister sure would have."

"I think she's a little scared of the woods right now," said Matthew as they crossed the side yard.

"Abby, you will never guess what I figured out last night," said Nick.

"I've got something to tell you, too!" said Abby. "I think I know what that rise in the woods is." Abby stopped at the fence and looked at the two boys.

"Indian mound," Nick and Abby said at the same time. Each looked toward the other, and together they said, "How did you know?"

As they climbed through the barbed-wire fence, Nick told Abby about his social studies project and visiting Poverty Point World Heritage Site.

"So that's how you knew that digging up artifacts was illegal," said Abby, standing up after climbing through the fence. She went on to explain how all the facts they had heard and seen and read seemed to point to the rise being an Indian mound. The three moved farther into the woods.

"Impressive logic, Abby," said Matthew.

"You been reading Sherlock Holmes? 'Elementary, my dear Watson,'" Nick teased.

Abby playfully punched Nick on the arm and then said, "See, I told you I was good at mysteries. Let's go take another look."

They approached the burned area in order to find the trail to the rise. The rain had smoothed the sandy soil in the cleared area around the burned logs. The acrid smell was gone. Matthew and Nick were beginning to walk around the burn site when Abby pointed to the ground. "Look, guys."

Footprints were clearly visible in the dirt.

"Looks like someone has been in the woods again," said Matthew with a grim look at the ground.

"Do you think they might still be here?" Abby asked, glancing around the woods.

"Don't worry; we're prepared. Right, Matt?" said Nick.

"What do you mean?" asked Abby.

Matthew unzipped the backpack and pulled out a pistol. Abby jumped back and stared at him.

"Don't worry, Abby. It's just a pellet gun," said Matthew.

"Yeah. It shoots BBs," said Nick.

Abby frowned at Nick. "I knew that." Looking back at Matthew, she said, "Do you know how to use that thing?"

"Yep. Dad showed me. He and I used to shoot at cans. He told me I could shoot a snake if one ever came into the yard."

"I *was* kind of wondering why you brought that backpack. I thought it might be to carry Nick's snacks."

Matthew grinned to himself and pretended to search the backpack. "Nothing here. Sorry, Nick."

Nick shrugged his shoulders, refusing to be riled. "We should plan for that in the future, actually."

"Let's follow the footprints. See where they go," said Matthew.

"Be careful not to mess them up. Walk outside the burned area, on the pine straw," said Abby.

Nick nodded. "That way we won't mess up any evidence."

The three walked around the outside of the burn site, looking at the footprints. The footprints went from the north side of the burned logs close to the house, around to the south side of the clearing. It looked like someone had walked around to the house side of the logs and back to the other side. If the three looked up, they could see the house between the trees.

"There's something drawn in the dirt. Over there, close to the logs," said Matthew, indicating an area between the burned logs and the house.

Abby grabbed Nick's arm as he started to walk toward the marks in the dirt and said, "You'll mess up the tracks."

"Then how am I supposed to see what that is?" Nick glared at Abby.

Abby shrugged. "Well, maybe just one of us should go. Less likely to mess up the evidence."

"I'll go," said Matthew. Abby and Nick watched as Matthew carefully walked to the right of the footprints until he reached the markings in the dirt, about six feet past Nick and Abby.

"What is it?" asked Nick.

"Is it words?" asked Abby.

"It's not words. It's a circle with figures in the middle." Matthew leaned over to get a better look at the drawing. "It looks like stick figures. I'm trying to figure out which way is up."

Abby and Nick strained to see the drawing from the pine straw at the edge of the clearing. The space was in the mottled shadows of the trees even though the morning sunshine shone brightly.

"What kind of figures?" asked Abby.

Matthew looked up at them. "I think you should come and look," he said seriously.

"Wait!" Abby grabbed Nick's arm before he started

toward Matthew. "Let's get a good look at where these footprints go before we move." She turned to look around the south edge of the clearing. "They look like a man's. Compare your foot, Nick." Nick carefully placed his foot beside one of the impressions in the dirt.

"Yeah, my feet aren't small and this one is bigger than my foot."

"The footprints go that way." Abby pointed to the wooded area opposite the house.

"Isn't that the way to the cabin at the end of the road?" asked Nick.

"Yeah," said Matthew, "it is."

The pair turned back and, careful to tread where Matthew had walked, joined him at the circle of figures. The picture was drawn in the ash from the fire, the lighter sandy soil showing through the markings in the dark ash. The circle containing the figures was about two feet in diameter.

The three looked closely at the figures. Abby tried to lean over and see the drawing from the other side.

"I see what you mean, Matt," she said. "I'm not sure which way is up either."

"It looks like people in the Indian drawings we saw in the books," said Matthew.

"Looks like that to me too," said Nick.

"In fact, it looks like a woman and two children, a boy and a girl," said Abby.

"Yep," muttered Matthew, with a worried sound in his voice. "Looking at it from the house side, the figures are upside down."

"Hey!" said Nick. "Do you think this is supposed to be you and your mom and sister?"

"That is what it looks like," said Abby.

"What do you think it means, Matt?"

Matthew could feel his anger rising. "I don't know but I'm going to find out!" He clinched his fists at his sides. "First the fire and now this. This makes me mad." He kicked at a black feather lying in the dirt at the edge of the drawing. "We have one of the Caddo Indian books here at the house. Let's see if it has any figures like these in it." Matthew took off for the house.

Abby and Nick hurried after him.

When the book didn't show any symbols like the ones drawn in the dirt, Abby said, "Let's go down to my grandparent's house and use the internet. I'll ask Grandma to feed us lunch."

The boys agreed and they headed down the blacktop road.

While they were waiting for lunch, they gathered around the computer desk in the den. The boys pulled dining room chairs behind Abby, who was in the desk chair.

"Try Googling 'Indian symbols,'" said Nick.

Abby frowned at him. "Nick, I think I know how to search on the internet."

"Just suggestin'," muttered Nick.

Abby typed in "North American Indian symbols" and several sites came up. She clicked on a couple before locating one that had a chart of symbols and their meanings. She scrolled down the list, looking for the figures. She found individual drawings of people similar to those they had found in the dirt. A little farther down the chart were figures of people surrounded by a circle. The figures were upside down in the circle.

"That looks like it," said Matthew.

After reading the description beside the symbol, Abby said, "Wow!" She turned suddenly to look at the two boys. "Read what this says, guys." She leaned back in her chair so they could get a better look at the small print on the screen. The boys leaned toward the desktop computer.

Nick whistled low between his teeth. "This is not good, Matt."

Matthew read the description again. "Go back up to the other ones showing just the stick figures." Abby scrolled back up to the other drawings of people.

He looked carefully at that description as well, then he sat back in his chair. "Those simply show the male and female symbols. The drawing with the figures in the circle looks more like the one we found in the dirt. The trouble is . . . Abby, would you go back to the very top of the page?"

He waited as Abby scrolled to the top of the site. "See, this site is for Indian symbols, all right, but the Caddo are not listed as one of the tribes that used these symbols."

Abby pointed to the books stacked on the coffee table. "Grab that book on top, Nick. Look in the index for 'symbols.'"

Nick reached across to the table for one of the Caddo Indian book and opened to the front. "The *index*, Nick, not the *table of contents*. It's in the back."

"Yeah, yeah, yeah," muttered Nick as he flipped to the back of the book. He found the listing and then turned to the correct page. The other two got up and leaned over his shoulder to look.

"No symbols like that in this book," said Nick as he flipped through the pages.

"But that doesn't mean they didn't use these," said Abby. "Mr. Jones said that most of what we know about the Caddo Indians is limited to what the European explorers recorded."

"And they did trade with other tribes," said Matthew.

"Well, then couldn't the Caddo have used this symbol? Don't you think they sometimes wanted those interfering European explorers dead?" said Nick emphatically.

Matthew saw Abby try to motion to Nick to be quiet.

"I know what it said, Abby," said Matthew quietly. "I know that if the figures are upside down, that meant 'death.' The drawing in the clearing is upside down if you look at it from the side toward the house."

"But, we're not sure that this is a symbol they used," said Abby. "I read more last night and discovered that they were a peaceful people. The Caddo Indians got along well with the explorers for a long time. They traded with them. That's where they got horses."

"I see what you're saying, Abby, but the fact is that someone drew that symbol in my woods."

Nick stood to face the other two. "I hate to state the obvious, guys . . ."

"But you will, won't you?" Abby tried to smile as she said this.

Nick scowled at her and said, "Matt, have you actually received any messages from someone threatening you or your mom and sister?"

Matthew hesitated. "I guess not." He stuck his hands in his shorts pockets.

"Has anyone actually come into your yard or your house?"

"Not that I know of."

"Then maybe it's like my dad says about animals in the wild—they are as afraid of you as you are of them."

"I see what you're saying, Nick," said Abby. "Whoever is doing this seems to be trying to scare you. By the way, Nick, that was very insightful."

Nick nodded at her and smiled.

Matthew considered this, pulled his hands out of his pockets, and then angrily replied, "They need to be more afraid of me than I am of them. I'm not giving in to their immature scare tactics. We were on our way to see the mound. I'm still determined to go."

"Me too, buddy!" said Nick.

"And me," said Abby.

Matthew felt a twinge of sadness with his anger. He hoped that his dad would be proud of his actions. It was left to him to protect his family.

Chapter 7

Wednesday afternoon, June 18

After ham sandwiches for lunch at the Stewards' house, the trio headed back to the Morin farmhouse. Heat waves rose off the blacktop road as they walked. Nick wiped his face with the tail of his t-shirt. Matthew noticed the hawk on a power line and thought again about his dad.

Back at the farmhouse, Matthew and the others found his mom and Kate in the front bedroom looking in the closet.

"What's all this?" Matthew asked, looking at the items splayed across the chenille bedspread. There were books, some items of clothing, and a small box.

"Your dad stored some of his keepsakes here, apparently," said Mom, coming out of the closet with an old Cub Scout shirt. "I found this stuff on the top shelf."

"This couldn't have been his," Matthew said, picking up a 1966 yearbook from the local high school.

"No, that would be your granddad's," said Mom.

"Let me see," said Abby. Matthew handed her the yearbook. "I wonder if my granddad is in there," Abby said, flipping through the yearbook.

"Look at this," said Kate. Turning from the window, she held up an old metal kaleidoscope.

"Oh, cool," said Nick. "Can I have a look?" He turned toward the window and rotated the lower section of the tin kaleidoscope. The bright colored shapes rearranged themselves into a new pattern.

Kate picked up a soft rubbery figure and said, "This doll feels funny."

"That's Stretch Armstrong. Try pulling his arms and legs," said Matthew. Kate pulled on the arms and laughed at how far they would stretch.

Matthew picked up a wooden box about six-inches square. "What's in here?"

"I haven't opened it yet. You can," said Mom.

From the box Matthew began pulling out items. "This is a Superior ribbon for a band performance," he said. Reaching back into the box, he held up a lapel pin, "This says 'Student Council,' and it has year bars attached, 1964 through 1967."

"Let me find the student council picture." Abby flipped through the yearbook and found the Student Council page. She pointed to a face in a picture. "This guy's name is Morin. Is that your granddad?"

"That's cool. He's much younger there and looks kinda like my dad."

"I want to see," said Kate, squeezing between Matthew and Abby. Abby lowered the book so Kate could look at the picture. Kate took the book and sat on a stool to look at it.

"I didn't know my granddad very well," said Matthew. "He died several years ago."

"Sorry," said Abby.

Matthew gave a small smile as thanks. "Hey, look at this!" Matthew said as he pulled what looked like a small stone from the box. It was flat and less than an inch long.

"What is it?" asked Nick as he looked around Matthew's shoulder.

"It looks like a tiny arrowhead," Matthew said, turning it over in his hand. "Dad or Granddad must have found it. Mom, that means there could be more. We really want to look for arrowheads again this afternoon since we didn't find any this morning."

"I still don't like this, Matthew," she said, coming out of the closet and folding her arms across her chest. "Where exactly did y'all go this morning?"

"Only to the burn site," said Matthew.

"And there are three of us, Mrs. M. We'll be careful and keep our eyes open," said Nick.

"We'll come right back if we see anything," added Abby.

"Can we go, Mom?" Matthew looked at Mom. "Please."

She hesitated with a worried look on her face but then looked at the three in front of her. She sighed. "Okay, I know your dad would have encouraged you. A little history and a little family. He would have approved."

"I want to go," said Kate, jumping up from her stool.

"You and I can look down by the lake," said Mom. She turned to the other three. "That way I can hear you if you call."

"That's great, Mom."

"Yeah, thanks, Mrs. Morin," added Abby.

"But Mommy . . ." said Kate.

"You can hold this for me as we look," Mom said, holding up a small basket. "We'll collect what we find in this."

Kate took the basket and looked inside.

As the trio ran down the hallway and out the front door, Matthew heard his mother holler, "Stay within calling distance!"

Matthew, Abby, and Nick ran down the front steps and angled for the woods.

The birds were making all kinds of noise that afternoon as the three approached the burned-log section. It was not only the regular singing of the mockingbirds, but also a squawking kind of noise. Matthew looked up and saw a crow watching them from a pine tree.

They took another quick look at the drawing in the dirt before Matthew grabbed a pine branch and brushed the image away. Somehow he felt better after the drawing was gone. He told himself that he didn't want Kate or his mom to find it.

"If my mom would let me get a cell phone, I could have taken a picture of that drawing," grumbled Nick. "You know, for reference later."

Abby and Matthew nodded. Then they turned toward the trail that led to the burial mound.

They had gone only about five feet toward the start of the trail at the edge of the woods when Matthew, who was leading the group, halted suddenly.

"Hey! Give a guy some notice if you're gonna stop short like that," complained Nick as he tried to avoid running into Matthew.

"Look," said Matthew in a whisper, pointing to the trail ahead.

Abby and Nick peered around each side of him.

"What are we looking at?" asked Nick. "Another drawing?"

"Look on the path beside that tree," said Abby quietly, pointing that way.

On the ground where the path led away from the cleared area was a coiled tan and black snake.

"I would have preferred another dirt drawing," muttered Nick.

"Back up slowly," whispered Matthew. He never took his eyes off the snake as the three retreated.

When they reached the north side of the burned area, Matthew said, "That's a rattlesnake."

Abby nodded. "Granddad showed me what to look for so I could recognize one."

"My dad showed me, too, but I don't think I have ever actually seen one before."

"Shoot it, Matt," said Nick.

He reached for the backpack but realized it wasn't hanging on his shoulder. "Oh, snap! I don't have the pellet gun. I left the backpack at the house."

From the safety of the far side of the burned logs, Nick asked, "What do we do now? Do these things travel in pairs?"

"I don't think so," said Matthew. "Let's watch and see what it does."

All three trained their eyes on the snake. The afternoon sun filtered through the tall pine trees and lay in dappled patches on the pine straw on the ground.

"It doesn't seem to be moving," Matthew said after a minute.

"I thought snakes liked to sun themselves. This is not very sunny," said Nick.

"Granddad says they prefer cool spots in hot weather, like under shrubs and logs." Abby's voice was still lowered.

"Then why is that one in the middle of the trail?" Nick cast a worried look at the burned logs as he backed farther away from them. "Why isn't he shaking his rattles at us?"

"Good question, Nick. Something feels wrong with this picture," said Matthew.

"Try throwing a stick at it," said Nick.

Abby rolled her eyes and shook her head.

"Well, it is way over there. Not like it could get us from this far away," said Nick.

"But it could go into the brush right beside the trail, and then how would we know where it was? We still couldn't go down the trail," Abby told him.

"Snakes are fast, Nick. We might not see where it went. And he's almost the same colors as the pine straw in this shady spot."

"Oh," Nick said. "So what do we do now?"

"Have y'all looked at its head? Does something look wrong with it?" asked Matthew.

"Do you think it's a mutant? That would be cool." Nick squinted at the snake.

"I don't think that's it," said Abby, "but I see what you mean, Matt." She started to walk closer to the snake.

"Wait, Abby," said Matthew, grabbing her arm as she walked past him. "At least I have on sneakers. You have on sandals. Not a good idea when a snake is around."

"Good point. You try for a closer look."

Matthew picked up a stick and tentatively approached

the snake, stopping a couple of yards away. He leaned in to see the head, which angled to the left. Then he straightened and walked toward the snake.

Both Abby and Nick asked, "What are you doing?!"

"It's okay. It's dead," he said. "Come look. This snake has been shot."

The other two walked up. They looked down at the snake as Matthew used the stick to raise its head.

"He's still got his head so it's been shot with a small caliber weapon," said Nick. "The shot was more of a glancing blow. A larger bullet could have blown his head right off."

Matthew and Abby looked at him in astonishment.

"What? Don't be so surprised. My dad and uncle have been taking me to the shooting range. And they took me hunting for the first time last fall."

"Oh, yeah. I remember that," said Matthew.

"I think this was a .22 caliber rifle or something small like that. That is what I was shooting with," said Nick.

"Did you shoot anything?" asked Abby. "When you went hunting, I mean?"

"I missed a squirrel," Nick admitted.

"Yeah, Granddad goes squirrel hunting." Abby looked closer at the snake. "Do you think this is the way the snake died, all curled up like this? Wouldn't the force of the shot knock it into some crazy shape or something?"

"Yeah, it would," said Nick.

Matthew stood up slowly and looked around. "Then someone put it here."

"Someone who didn't want us going down this trail," said Abby.

"All the more reason for us to go," said Matthew, planting his stick on the ground like a wizard's staff.

"I refuse to be scared off by a dead snake," said Nick, standing tall and striking a superhero pose.

"Yeah! We will not be scared off," said Abby, raising her fist in the victory pose.

"Whoever is doing this will not stop me from getting another look at that rise," said Matthew.

"We need to see if the hill looks like an Indian mound," said Nick.

"Let's go." Matthew moved the snake off the path with the stick and the group moved past it.

"So, Nick," said Abby as she moved in line on the trail behind him, "didn't your dad and uncle warn you about snakes in the woods when y'all went hunting?"

"Yeah, but they said I was making so much noise that I'd scared all the snakes away. And the deer. And the squirrels. And probably the bears if there had been any around."

Matthew and Abby laughed at Nick's confession.

As they walked down the trail, Matthew felt a little pang of guilt about hiding all these events from his mother. But he was determined not to tell her—at least, not yet. He didn't want to scare her. He wanted to handle this problem like he thought Dad would have.

Plus, he was angry at someone for thinking he was just a kid like his little sister. He was not going to be scared off.

He kept sharp eyes on the woods as they continued down the trail. The group came out of the trees and into the open area around the rise. Matthew was relieved that they hadn't seen any more snakes or strange movements in the woods. He was thankful for the help of his friends, especially this new one, but he didn't want them hurt.

They walked to the middle of the rise. Abby scrambled down and stepped away toward the woods to look back at the area. Nick walked around to the lake side of the small hill, mumbling to himself as he went.

"Find something, Nick? Or is that your stomach I hear grumbling?" Matthew said.

"I was repeating some of the characteristics of a burial mound. This looks like what I wrote my report about. It's about the right size and shape."

"I agree," said Abby from the other side. "It rises straight out of the ground without any other hills around."

"You know, we may have discovered an Indian mound that had been forgotten." Nick's voice rose as he continued to inspect the rise.

"It goes along with what Mr. Charlie said about this being an old Indian community," Matthew said.

"I think that some mounds were built at the edge of Indian towns," said Nick.

"And remember that Mr. Jones said that they found one at Belcher on the Red River a few years ago," said Matthew. "I'm impressed, Nick. You really did learn something from that project."

Nick shrugged his shoulders. "I'm not an ignoramus. I just don't like to study."

"This is too creepy. Look at all that's happened." Abby held up her hand and counted on her fingers. "The woods mysteriously catch on fire. We find an Indian drawing and a mound in these woods. Plus a Caddo Indian now lives on the other side of these woods. This is too much for coincidence."

"And," said Matthew, "a couple of times since we got here last week, I have seen something in these woods."

Nick and Abby both turned and stared at Matthew. He shrugged.

"The first time was the day we got here. I thought it was a bird or something. Now I wonder."

"You hadn't told us that, Matt," said Abby.

Matthew kicked a pine cone with his sneaker. "It didn't seem to be important until you mentioned all that other evidence and thought you saw someone yesterday."

Abby glanced around at the trees.

"Do you think that man from the cabin is watching you?" asked Nick, also glancing toward the woods. "Why would he do that?"

"Maybe it has something to do with this mound," said Abby.

"Yeah, maybe he doesn't want you looking into this. He

wants this mound for himself." Nick's voice raised and his hands made themselves into fists.

Matthew frowned. "This mound is on *my* land—well, my family's land. We have a right to look at it."

"Let's check all around it," Abby said, nodding at Matthew's comment.

Nick and Abby checked the sides. Matthew walked toward the far end of the rise. He stooped and stared at a hole about the size of a soccer ball he saw at the base of the rise. The rain had settled the small amount of dug-out red dirt. Matthew leaned over for a closer look, but he couldn't tell if the digging had been done by an animal or a human.

He stooped to pick up something in the dirt and walked toward the others.

"I really think we are right about this mound, Matt," said Abby, standing with her hands on her hips, looking at the rise. Then she walked around to the lake side. "That would explain why I thought someone had piled the dirt here."

"I think y'all are right. At the other end I found a hole where something or someone has been digging. The rain has settled the dirt too much to tell what dug it out."

"A dug-out spot! Where?" said Abby.

They hurried to the south end of the rise and looked at the hole Matthew had found. Abby looked around the opening, moving the pine straw away.

Nick squatted. "Nothing else in the hole," Nick said. "Could it have been an animal digging? Like a squirrel burying an acorn?"

"I don't think squirrels leave their holes dug out like that. They want their acorns hidden," said Matthew.

"Yeah, I guess you're right," Nick said. Then he added, "What I wouldn't give to dig into this mound and find what's in it."

"Well, it is on Matt's family's land," Abby said. "Why can't we do that?"

"I don't think that's allowed," said Nick.

"I guess it would be kind of like digging into a person's grave," she said.

"I also found this." Matthew held out an almost perfect arrowhead. It was about one and a half inches long and chipped from a dark gray stone. "I guess the digging and the rain uncovered it."

"Sweet. Let me see." Nick reached for the arrowhead and Matthew handed it to him. "This is so cool. You can see the nicks in the stone where it was shaped and sharpened. I'm going to look around some more."

They scouted the area around the mound for several minutes, occasionally kicking pine straw aside and stooping for a closer look.

"There don't seem to be any other signs of an Indian community here. No pottery shards or shells," said Abby.

"Wouldn't that have been like a hundred years ago?" asked Nick.

"More like a thousand," Matthew said. "The signs were probably gone even before my great-great grandparents settled here." He looked between the trees toward the lake down the ridge. "I wonder why the Caddo left this area. Who knows, they might have been the same ones who lived beside the Red River."

With eyebrows knitted together, Abby said, "But what I don't get about this mound is how it survived being on farmland."

"All I know is that the land on this side of the house, the south side, was pasture for cows. Dad told me that his family planted these pine trees when they sold off the cows. Selling some of those trees for pulp wood is going to help pay for my college."

"I guess there wouldn't have been any plowing up of the dirt around the mound since this was a pasture. So any buried arrowheads are probably still buried. That's why we are not finding anything."

"I'm glad you found this one," said Nick, handing the arrowhead back to Matthew. "This is so awesome. I like history."

"This is a first," said Matthew, slipping the arrowhead into his shorts pocket. "Nick is interested in something from school besides lunch."

Nick picked up a pine cone and threw it at him. Immediately the battle ensued. All three ran around, hiding behind trees, throwing pine cone grenades.

After a while, Abby stopped, stepped out from behind a tree, and was instantly bombarded with pine cones from both boys. Holding her hands in front of her face, she yelled, "Hey, guys, truce! Truce!"

After the pine cones stopped, she said, "I was thinking. Since we are this far into the woods, maybe we should go and take a look at that cabin."

Matthew frowned slightly at Abby's suggestion. What if the man saw them? He didn't want his mom and sister in danger.

"I don't know, Abby," said Matthew. "It doesn't feel right going onto someone else's land."

"We could scout it out from the edge of the trees," said Nick.

"What are we looking for?" asked Matthew. "Do you think he has a sign in his yard telling us he set the fire?"

"I think it's a good idea, Matt," said Abby, looking steadily at Matthew. "I'm going even if you don't."

"Come on, Matt. We *do* need to find out something about him. We will only look, not go up to the cabin or anything like that."

"Well, there is an old fence that marks the edge of our land. We could go that far. I think we could probably see the cabin from there. The area around the cabin used to be grown up with brambles and small trees, but Mr. Charlie seemed to think that the man has been cutting all that out to make a yard."

Abby and Nick started moving in the direction of the cabin. Matthew glanced back in the direction of his house and then said, "Let's try to be quiet and keep a lookout, okay."

The other two nodded in agreement.

They were soon standing at the fence. It was closer than Matthew had realized. The mound must be about half way between the Morin house and the cabin.

They peered over the barbed-wire fence, leaning to see between the few scattered trees toward the clearing. Grass was beginning to grow around the wood-frame cabin. A small porch was attached to the front of the cabin and two small wooden outbuildings stood behind. Parked in the dirt driveway was a green Ford truck. Nice truck, Matthew thought to himself, and then he felt foolish to be thinking about trucks at a time like this.

"Well, he has electricity," said Nick. "I see lines running to the house, but why are the lines also going to the other buildings?"

"Those two buildings are probably the pump house and a toolshed," said Matthew. "We also need electricity to run our pump to get water from the well under our pump house."

"That's cool," said Nick, then he turned to Abby. "You have a well under your pump house?"

"Yeah. My granddad has an old pump house too," said Abby. "Let's look for anything strange. Something that doesn't belong."

Suddenly a dark-haired man appeared from behind the tool shed. All three kids ducked.

Matthew could see that the man held a bowl in one hand, but he wasn't sure what was in the other. He gasped when he realized what it was.

"What's he holding?" asked Abby.

"That," stated Matthew, "is a snake skin."

"Oh, my gosh!" said Nick, a little too loudly. "Then it must be him!"

"Shush," said Matthew and Abby.

"That's the man I saw at the library last night!" Matthew whispered.

The man entered the toolshed. "Let's get out of here," said Matthew. Crouching low, he moved back into the shadows of the pine woods and hoped that the others were following.

They made their way back through the woods, passing the rise and skirting the burn site, then they ducked through the barbed-wire fence. Walking across the yard, they were surprised to see Mr. Charlie sitting with Mom on the porch. Both of the adults turned to watch the three approach the porch. Mr. Charlie was not smiling.

"I hear you children have been spendin' a good bit of time in these woods," he said as they came up the steps.

"Yes, sir," said Abby. "We thought we could look for Indian arrowheads. You got me really interested in them when you said there used to be a town around here. And look, Matt found one."

Matthew handed the arrowhead to Mr. Charlie.

"That's a nice one," Mr. Charlie said, handing it back to Matthew, "but Matt's mom and I have had a little conversation, and we think it's best that y'all stay out of the woods for now."

"But why, Mr. Charlie?" said Matthew. "We're staying on our land, and we want to look for more arrowheads."

"Yeah, Mr. Steward, we even got books from the library about the Caddo Indians to help in our hunt," said Nick.

"I know y'all are real interested in this stuff. Abby, your grandma told me y'all checked out the books, but there are things you don't know," said Mr. Charlie firmly. "You need to stay here or up at our house for the next few days."

"Why, Granddad?" asked Abby.

"Was there another fire?" asked Nick.

Mr. Charlie just shook his head but didn't answer their questions.

"Matthew, I wholeheartedly agree with Mr. Charlie. You need to stay around here and out of the woods for a while," said Mom.

"Something else must have happened," muttered Abby.

"Now, you don't need to worry about that," said Mr. Charlie. "We want you to stay out of the woods. And Abby, if you want to come down here to visit, ask me or your grandma to drive you."

"Matthew, same goes for you and Nick. I can drive you to the Stewards' if you want to go up there. You need to stay off the road and out of the woods."

The three kids looked at each other. Matthew figured they were all thinking the same thing: Something was definitely different.

He thought about the dead snake. Someone wanted to scare them. If it was originally Indian land, maybe Nick was right; maybe the mysterious man in the cabin thought it ought to be Indian land again.

CHAPTER 8

THURSDAY, JUNE 19

The next day, Matthew and Nick tried to play *Flying Eagles*, but Matthew was distracted. Since Nick kept missing easy shots, Matthew guessed he was having trouble concentrating as well. So they looked through the Caddo Indian book again but didn't gain any insight into what they had seen in the woods.

Matthew could hear Mom in the hallway, coming down the stairs from the attic. Last year, Matthew had asked his dad about why they had stairs rather than a pull down door for the attic. His dad had said that the stairs allowed easy access to the attic because they had used it for all kinds of storage, including canned food, and even as a place to hang laundry when it was raining.

Mom called to the two boys to join her in the dining room. "Come look at this old photo album. I think it's from the time when your dad's great-grandparents first settled this land."

"Nick," whispered Matt, "maybe it has pictures of the pasture or the mound." Nick nodded and they joined his mother and Kate at the dining room table.

The leather-bound album was about two inches thick with black pages. Little pieces of the slightly brittle paper broke off like black confetti as Matthew's mom opened the album. The old black-and-white photographs were mounted with corner tabs. Most showed scenes of the house and farm. One picture showed a view of an old barn and some cows. Another showed row after row of the tall corn-like stalks of a sugarcane field. In another photo the cut sugarcane had been placed into large piles of cane stalks ready for processing. There was one photograph with a boy feeding cane stalks into an old press mill with a mule in the background. Matthew recognized the old spout at the base of the mill—the one Mr. Charlie had showed him in the toolshed. A boy about his age was in another photo holding a stalk of sugarcane up to his mouth.

"What's he doing?" Matthew asked, pointing to the boy.

"He was probably chewing on a stalk of sugarcane," she answered.

"What?" asked Nick.

"Eww. Is that like chewing a stick?" asked Kate.

"No. It's sweet. You cut a small piece of cane and chew it to get out the sweet juice," she said. "Then you spit out the stalk."

"I still think that sounds nasty," said Kate, scrunching up her face.

Another photo showed a group of people posed on the front porch of a house. The steps looked similar to the ones on their front porch but the house looked different. The old brick sidewalk went straight to the steps.

"What house is that?" asked Matthew.

"I'm not sure," Mom answered. "These photos are older than the 1940s when this present house was built."

When Mom turned the page, Matthew looked with surprise at the next image. Nick jabbed Matthew's arm and pointed at the photo. A man who looked a lot like Matthew's dad stood beside a man who had dark hair hanging past his shoulders. In the background was the mound. The stumps from cleared trees were around the men. Both men were holding axes.

Matthew had a strange feeling that someone was looking over his shoulder. He thought Kate must have come up behind him, but when he turned to look, she was still sitting on the other side of Mom.

The remaining photographs showed people on the porch

and in the yard. One showed a large dinner on the grounds. Boards had been placed over sawhorses to make a long table, which was loaded with dishes of food. People in dress clothes, some holding plates, stood behind the table, sat on benches, or sat on the porch. No other photographs showed the field or the mound again, but that one photo seemed to indicate that his relatives had known about the mound in the early years of the farm.

After lunch Matthew and Nick sat on the front porch. Nick used his Croc-clad foot to push on the floor to start the swing. Matthew propped his sneakers on the table between the rocking chairs. They were rehashing everything when they saw the green truck go past the house. The man inside waved to them. Matthew watched the truck as it passed the house going toward the Stewards'.

"Was that him—Caddo Indian Cabin Man?" asked Nick, turning sideways and propping his feet on the porch swing.

"I guess so."

"He certainly was friendly."

"Maybe he's trying to throw us off the trail," said Matthew.

"How long has Caddo Indian Cabin Man been living down the road?"

"You like calling him that?" said Matthew with a laugh.

"Well, we don't have another name for him, do we?"

"He's been there for about three months, I guess."

"I wonder if he's kin to that man we saw in the photo, the one in front of the mound," said Nick.

"That would explain why he's here. His family must still own that land," said Matthew.

"I wish we could get a look inside his cabin while he's gone."

"Nick, we don't even know what to look for!"

"It's like my dad says about hunting—keep your eyes open and your mouth shut."

"It's a lost cause right now. We can't go out of the yard, much less down the road or back into the woods."

"Matt, we just gotta find a way." Nick put his feet back on the floor and leaned toward Matthew. "It looks like your great-grandfather—"

"Great-great-grandfather," Matthew corrected.

"Whatever. Anyway it looks like he knew about the mound. Why else would he have taken that picture with that other man? I think your mom is planning to take me home this weekend. This is Thursday. Time is running out."

Matthew looked up at the sound of a car thumping across the cattle guard. It was a red Acura, his uncle's car. Matthew hopped out of the rocking chair.

"How's it going, buddy?" the man called as he got out of his car.

"Uncle Roy! What are you doing here?"

"I thought I'd have a long weekend." He got his suitcase out of the trunk and walked toward the porch steps. "Who's your friend?"

"This is Nick," Matthew said as he hugged his uncle.

"Nice to meet you, Nick," Uncle Roy said as he shook Nick's hand.

"And you, sir," answered Nick.

Mom came onto the porch followed by Kate. "Roy, I'm so glad you could come. Jan couldn't come with you?" she said as she crossed the porch.

"Hello, Miss Kate," Uncle Roy said as he gave Kate a hug. "No, Jan said to tell you she would miss seeing you. She has a church meeting on Saturday—a women's conference. She helped plan it and said she wouldn't feel right missing it."

"That makes sense," Mom said, but she seemed distracted. "I'm glad you came Roy, especially since Dan's not . . ." She straightened her shoulders and then put a smile on her face. "I've got the front bedroom ready for you. Kate's moved into my room."

She looked at Matthew. "Will you grab Uncle Roy's suitcase?"

"I'll get it," said Kate and started to scrape the suitcase across the porch floor.

Uncle Roy laughed and picked up the suitcase. "Thanks, but I can get it." He followed Mom and Kate into the house.

Matthew and Nick looked at each other.

In a low voice, Matthew said, "Did you hear what Mom said? Uncle Roy didn't come for a long weekend. I think Mom asked him to come. He had to come all the way from Dallas."

"Whew. We know that Mr. Steward and your mom were discussing something when we came out of the woods yesterday. They are definitely keeping secrets from us."

"How can we find out what it is? I don't think that either Mom or Mr. Charlie is going to tell us."

Looking sideways at Matthew with narrowed eyes, Nick said, "We may have to use some subterfuge."

Matthew looked at him in surprise.

"Well, that was one of our vocabulary words. I do learn things, you know. Matt, we need an adult on our side." He pushed his foot against the porch floor and started the swing, with a determined look on his face.

Shortly afterwards, Uncle Roy came onto the porch. "Hey, guys. Can't find anything to do?"

"We were looking for arrowheads, but now Mom won't let us go back in the woods."

"I heard, Matt. I know you're disappointed."

"There was a small arrowhead in a box that Mom found in the front bedroom closet," said Matthew. "Did you find that one in the woods?"

"No. Must be your dad's. Later we can look for the box of arrowheads in the attic."

"There's a box of arrowheads in the attic?" asked Matthew, surprised. "Did you find those?"

"Actually, my grandfather's father found them when he started clearing the field over there south of the house." Uncle Roy pointed to the woods where the fire and the mound were located.

Matthew and Nick looked at each other knowingly, and

then Matthew said, "So they knew that Indians used to live on this land?"

"That's the story I heard when I was even younger than you."

"So how far did the pasture go? Did it go from the road to the lake?" Matthew asked.

"I seem to remember that it did. Then a number of years ago, after my grandfather quit farming and sold off the cattle, the pasture was planted in pine trees."

Matthew had been hoping to hear something about the mound, but Uncle Roy was walking toward the steps. "Why don't you fellows go fishing on the dock?"

"We already did that," said Nick.

"You'll find something to do. I'll see you later." He started down the steps.

"Where're you going?" Matthew asked.

"To town. I have an errand to run."

"Can we go with you?" asked Nick, with a quick "help-me-here" look at Matthew.

"Yeah," said Matthew. "Uh . . . we could get pizza."

"That sounds good! We haven't had pizza all week," said Nick.

Uncle Roy hesitated and then said, "Okay. Come on. Matt, run in and tell your mom. And tell her we'll bring pizza back."

On the way into town, after answering Uncle Roy's questions about school and summer so far, Matthew said, "Why won't they let us go back in the woods, Uncle Roy? Is Mom worried because of the fire? Or maybe something else has happened. Why did Mom call you to come all the way from Dallas? You've got to be up front with us."

"Yeah, us guys have to stick together," Nick said, leaning forward from the back seat. "They must think we're a bunch of babies. But we aren't, sir. We have been investigating this matter ourselves." Nick was trying to sound grown up.

"Nick!" exclaimed Matthew.

"It's okay, Matt. I think we can trust your uncle. Right, sir?"

"Why don't you boys tell me what you have been doing?" Uncle Roy said. He looked like he was trying not to smile.

For the next few minutes Matthew and Nick told him about their search of the burned area. They mentioned the man in the cabin and their research into the Caddo Indians. They explained their discovery of the mound.

"We're not sure why someone is trying to scare us. Maybe they're trying to get us to leave," Matthew said.

"So, your request to look for arrowheads was just an excuse to get back into the woods?" Uncle Roy asked.

"Yes, sir. We admit it," said Nick.

"We really wanted to get another look at that mound," said Matthew.

"Do you think that Caddo Indian Cabin Man wants to run us off?" said Nick.

"Who?" asked Uncle Roy with a laugh.

"That's Nick's name for the man who moved into the cabin."

"I don't know anything about that, Nick," said Uncle Roy, "but y'all think that you've found an Indian mound?"

"Yes, sir. I did a school project on mounds last year," said Nick.

"And after we read about them, we went back to the site to check it out," said Matthew. "It has all the characteristics."

"I have to admit that I'm impressed with your efforts so far."

"I'm trying to do what I think Dad would have wanted," said Matthew in a low voice.

Uncle Roy looked at Matthew beside him in the front seat but didn't comment. "And you, Nick?" he said, looking at Nick in his rear view mirror. "I think you like the adventure." Matthew turned to look at Nick in the back seat.

Nick smiled and nodded his head a little bit. "And don't forget Abby. She's been helping us too."

"Who's Abby?" asked Uncle Roy.

"Mr. Charlie's granddaughter," Matthew said. "She's visiting."

"Oh, yeah. They have a son who lives in Tyler."

"So what's going on?" Matthew asked.

"That's what I'm trying to find out. I'm headed to town to talk to Deputy Ramsey at the sheriff's substation. I want to get his take on this latest happening." He glanced at them as if to make a decision. "Someone shot at Charlie yesterday."

"What?!" said Nick.

"Shot at him?!" said Matthew.

"Well, really, someone shot over his head."

"Where did this happen?" asked Matthew.

"Did they shoot at him at his house?" asked Nick.

"Not exactly," said Uncle Roy. "Charlie went into the woods across from his house—adjacent to the woods on the right side of our house. He thought he saw someone when he took a letter out to the mailbox yesterday morning. He walked as far into the woods as that low area around the creek."

"Oh, yeah. That creek is in the woods on the other side of the house," Matthew told Nick.

"Charlie didn't see anyone, but he must have gotten too close for comfort. A shot went over his head. Charlie said the shot sounded like a .22 caliber rifle."

Matthew and Nick looked at each other. "Uh, I think I left out part of the story, Uncle Roy."

"You're not going to believe this, sir," added Nick, his voice sounding higher than usual.

Matthew told him about finding the dead rattlesnake. "We think someone put it there to keep us from going down the trail."

"A rattlesnake? Someone sure went to a lot of trouble to find a snake, shoot it, and then put it on the trail."

"I think it was shot with a twenty-two," said Nick. "My dad's been teaching me to shoot. I don't think this is a coincidence that someone shot at Mr. Steward with the same caliber."

Uncle Roy smiled at Nick's observation. "I'm glad that y'all told me about this. You have given me even more to talk to the deputy about." The car reached the edge of town, passing the high school.

"But, Uncle Roy, why didn't Mr. Charlie call the sheriff when he knew someone shot at him?"

"Yeah, and right there close to his house?" asked Nick emphatically.

"He did," Uncle Roy said. "Not much they could do. No one was there by the time the deputy got there. Then Charlie went down to the house to get Abby. Y'all must have come out of the woods right after Charlie finished explaining to your mom what had happened. He was just about to come looking for you."

Roy pulled the car into a parking place on a downtown street. The sheriff's substation was in an old bank building on the main street of the small town. Several other businesses in older-style storefront buildings lined both sides of the street.

Uncle Roy hesitated and turned to face the boys. "I know you guys are really interested in this, but I think you'd better let me talk to Deputy Ramsey without you."

"But . . ." both boys started to say.

Uncle Roy interrupted them, "I need Deputy Ramsey to talk straight with me, but he's going to look at you as kids. He won't talk as freely as he will if it's just me." He pulled a bill from his wallet. "Here's a five. Go get a Coke or something in the drugstore. I'll fill you in later."

A few minutes later, Matthew and Nick were perched on the red vinyl-covered stools at the lunch counter in the drugstore. The counter was black, rimmed with chrome, and the stool bases were chrome. Matthew looked around at the display of greeting cards and the old Coco-Cola tub of iced drinks. This old drugstore looked like it was stuck in the 1950s. He and Dad had come here often for old-fashioned hamburgers. Not many stores like this anymore, Dad had told him.

"Do you think he'll actually tell us what they talk about?" Nick asked, bringing Matthew back to the present. Nick took a sip of his milkshake. The glass mugs holding the milkshakes were frosty with the cold drink inside.

"I hope so. Someone may have tried to scare us with a dead snake, but they shot at Mr. Charlie." Matthew stirred his milkshake with his straw.

"Well, actually over his head," said Nick. Nick used his thumb to scrape some of the frosted area off his glass.

Watching Nick, Matthew told him, "Does that really matter? Someone was in my woods with a rifle. In my own woods!"

"So, are you giving up, Matt? Do you want to sit on the porch and wonder what's going on?" Nick turned on his stool to face Matthew.

Matthew looked at Nick and then turned back to his drink. "Actually I'm kind of surprised that Mom hasn't packed up and taken us back home by now. Especially after Mr. Charlie told her about the shooting."

"Well, she did call your Uncle Roy. Maybe she's trying to protect the house but needed help." Nick slurped the last of his milkshake.

The door of the drugstore opened and Uncle Roy walked up behind them. "Hey, guys, ready to go?"

"What'd you find out?" Matthew asked as he jumped off stool.

"Yeah, what's he going to do?" Nick asked, getting off his stool and trailing the other two out of the drugstore.

"We'll talk later. Right now, let's get pizza," Uncle Roy said.

"Do you suppose we could pick up Abby on our way back?" Matthew said. "She'll want to know what you found out."

Roy stopped on the sidewalk outside the store and looked at Matthew. "You are wading into deep water now, Matt.

Charlie didn't tell his granddaughter about the shooting. It's not our place to tell her. I need to respect his decision," said Uncle Roy. He continued to walk closer to his car and then turned back. "But we can share our pizza with her."

With hot pizza boxes on the back seat beside Nick, they drove back toward the farmhouse. Twenty minutes later they had picked up Abby and were all at the dining table, wolfing down pepperoni and Canadian-bacon pizzas.

"Matt, you didn't get cheese. You know I like cheese," said Kate.

"Just pull the pepperoni off," said Matthew. "You are so spoiled."

"No, I'm not," said Kate with pouting lips.

"All right, you two. Stop fussing," said Mom. "Kate, you like the Canadian bacon. Get that."

"Little sisters!" Nick said. "You got a little sister, Abby?"

"Nope. I am the little sister!"

"That explains a lot," Nick said, smiling at Abby's pretend-upset expression.

When all the boxes were empty, Matthew, Abby, and Nick lingered at the table while the others went into the living room. Matthew and Nick updated Abby concerning Uncle Roy and that afternoon's visit with the deputy. Matthew was conflicted about telling Abby about the reason the adults had told them not to go into the woods. She was in this with them after all, but he knew he was supposed to respect Mr. Charlie's decision not to tell her about the shooting.

"I can't get anything out of Granddad," said Abby. "All he would say was that someone had been shooting across the road. That's why he doesn't want us in the woods. We sometimes hear rifles when it's hunting season, but this is June! He seems really concerned."

"Wouldn't you be if someone shot at you?" said Nick.

With widened eyes, Abby looked at Nick and then Matthew. "What?!"

"Shhh!" Matthew said, looking behind him toward the

living room. Nick, once again, had jumped the gun, so to speak, without Matthew's knowing he would. But the secret was out now. Probably better for her to know. He told Abby about someone shooting at her granddad. "Don't tell that we told you. I think your granddad didn't want to scare you."

"But I need to know," said Abby in a hoarse whisper. "We need the facts. We can't figure this out without all the evidence. And this definitely puts a different spin on things. Until now, Matt, all the happenings were on your land. Now things seem to have spread."

"They must have been down by the creek. It runs through both properties," Matthew said.

Abby nodded her head thoughtfully and said, "What did the deputy tell your Uncle Roy?"

"We don't know," said Matthew, mindlessly pushing the empty pizza box across the table.

"He hasn't told us yet," said Nick pushing the box back to Matthew.

"Abby, we saw a truck drive up the road this morning. The man driving waved at us."

"Was it that green truck?" asked Abby.

"Yeah."

"I saw it too. I was helping Grandma water the flowers on the front porch. He waved at us too." Abby pushed the other box toward Nick.

"Did you get a good look at him?" Nick gave the box a shove back to Abby.

"Not really. He had dark hair like the man we saw at the cabin. That's all I could see."

"I'm positive it was Caddo Indian Cabin Man," said Nick.

Abby's brow furrowed a bit as she looked at Matthew.

"That's what Nick is calling the man who moved into the cabin," said Matthew. "Didn't your granddad say that he had seen him drive by before?"

"Yeah, but I don't think we can get any more details out of Granddad right now."

Then Uncle Roy and Mom walked into the dining room. "I put on a DVD for Kate to watch," said Mom. "We need to talk. I understand that y'all have been very busy."

Matthew knew that he couldn't hide things from his mom any longer. The group had a long talk around the dining room table. First, Matthew, Abby, and Nick told the grown-ups almost all of what they had done and discovered. Matthew watched the expressions on his mom's face alternate between surprise and concern.

He held back the information about the drawing in the dirt. It seemed almost too terrible to mention.

Abby told them that her grandfather had mentioned the rifle shots in the woods. She didn't say that she knew that the shooting was at her granddad. Then, Uncle Roy told about his meeting with Deputy Ramsey.

"Deputy Ramsey said that there haven't been any other complaints, but he would make note of everything we are worried about, including your suspicions concerning the Indian mound. He looked very thoughtful when I told him that."

"Is that all? Can't the sheriff's department at least patrol this road?" asked Mom. She sounded frustrated.

"He did say they would do that, especially because of the shots fired in the woods. Don't be worried if you see a sheriff's car turning around in the driveway."

"They're not going to the end of the road to look at the cabin, too?" said Matthew.

"No," said Uncle Roy. "Doug said that our driveway is easier to turn around in. The road leads straight into Mr. Washington's drive. The deputy didn't want to go into his yard to turn around."

"Is that Cabin Man's name?" asked Abby.

"Oh, yeah, I remember. The deputy mentioned his name after the fire," said Matthew. "So they're not going to check him out? What if he is the one responsible for all of this?"

"He might want y'all off this land because it was once his

ancestor's land," said Nick. "Or maybe burial land."

"Deputy Ramsey said that Mr. Washington has not reported any problems."

"Well, he wouldn't have if he was the one causing the problems!" said Nick.

"He didn't seem to have any suspicions about him, Nick," Uncle Roy said. "He did say that any deputy patrolling the area can see all the way to the end of the road from our drive."

"Is that all we can do?" asked Matthew.

"We can contact the archaeology department of one of the local universities to see if they want to check out the mound. It seems there had been some digs in northwest Louisiana several years ago by professors from Centenary College and Northwestern State."

"I still think it's strange that we never had any kind of trouble before this man moved into the cabin," said Matthew accusingly.

Mom looked at him and said pointedly, "Then isn't that another reason to stay out of the woods?"

He frowned. Mom would not understand why he felt he must find out what was happening in the woods. He knew that someone was trying to scare them off, but they had not really tried to harm anyone.

At least not so far.

Matthew felt that strange sensation of someone else being in the room again. He thought maybe Kate had come into the room to see what they were doing, but turning around, he didn't see her. Matthew tried to shrug off the feeling.

Uncle Roy asked, "Have any of you noticed any strange vehicles on this road?"

"Only that green truck that passed this morning," said Matthew.

"That one belongs to Mr. Washington. Deputy Ramsey told me about that truck when he asked us to keep an eye out for any others."

"We'll keep our eyes open," said Abby.

"And our mouths shut," said Nick.

Matthew grinned at Nick's inside joke.

"Time to take you home, Abby," said Uncle Roy as he rose from his chair.

"I'll see y'all in the morning," Abby said as she left the room. Matthew and Nick muttered their goodbyes.

It had gotten dark outside and, as Matthew got up from the table to throw away the pizza boxes, he glanced out the window in the direction of the fire site. For a second, he thought he saw a flash of light in the woods. He kept looking in that direction, but he didn't see it again.

Later in their bedroom after everyone had gone to bed, Matthew couldn't sleep. He got that feeling again that someone else was in the room with them. He grabbed the flashlight he kept under the bed and shined it around the room.

"What're you doing?" asked Nick.

"Thought I heard something," said Matthew. He didn't want to try to explain his funny feeling.

"See anything?"

"Nope." He hesitated a few seconds. "But I saw a flash of light in the woods after Abby left."

"What?" Nick sat up suddenly. "You think someone was in the woods? Why didn't you say something?"

"Well, I kind of thought it might be my imagination running away with me," said Matthew. "Now, I'm not so sure."

"Let's go look out the dining room window," said Nick. "We'll keep the lights off so we can see out better."

The boys crept down the hallway, trying to avoid the creaking floorboards, especially by the other bedroom doors. Matthew hoped they could get across the dining room without bumping into one of the chairs. There was only a dim glow of moonlight outside, but they could see well enough in the glow of appliances from the kitchen.

There were two windows in the dining room that looked

out to the woods on the south side of the house. Matthew crept over to one window and Nick to the other. They didn't see anything. But they heard something.

Creaking floorboards got their attention, but the sounds were not coming from inside the house. The creaks were on the front porch.

Another dining room window looked onto the front yard. Matthew silently motioned for Nick to join him at that window, but the boys couldn't see onto the porch because of the shrubs.

Nick motioned for them to go to the living room window that looked out onto the porch. Matthew tried to tiptoe quietly into the adjacent room. He and Nick squeezed behind the chair at the front window. Matthew slowly pulled back the curtain a crack. The boys peered out, Matthew's head above Nick's. Matthew could barely make out a dark shape in the moonlight running across the yard from the porch toward the woods. He looked down at Nick and whispered, "You see that?"

"Yeah!" said Nick. "Go!"

Matthew was not worried now about the noise they might make as both boys scrambled to the front door and onto the porch. They were just in time to see the dark form climb over the barbed-wire fence and disappear into the woods.

About that time, a flashlight beam hit them. Matthew and Nick both jumped and looked back at the front door.

Uncle Roy stood in the doorway in his pajama bottoms with a rifle and a flashlight in his hands. He held his finger to his lips and joined them on the porch, quietly closing the door as he came out. "What's going on?" he said in a quiet voice.

Matthew leaned his head toward his uncle and whispered, "I thought I saw a light in the woods earlier tonight, so we came to check it out."

"You know, with the lights out so we could see better," said Nick.

"Why didn't you get me?" asked Uncle Roy.

"If it wasn't anything, we didn't want to bother you," Matthew said sheepishly.

"And why are you on the porch? I heard the front door open from my room."

"Because we saw him!" said Nick.

"We saw someone running from the porch to the woods. He must have climbed over the fence." Matthew pointed to the woods to the south, the same direction as the fire site and Mr. Washington's cabin. "That's when you came out."

Uncle Roy looked toward the woods. "I don't see anything now. Could it have been a raccoon or a cat? They both like to roam at night."

"It looked bigger than a cat or a raccoon," said Matthew. "And we heard him on the front porch."

"What if it was an Indian spirit from the mound?" said Nick. "Maybe we are on sacred Indian ground."

"Now you're letting your imagination get the better of you," Uncle Roy said, shaking his head. "I'm going to walk over there and shine the flashlight into the woods to see if I can see anything. You two stay here."

As he approached the steps, one foot did a funny moving motion, swinging forward like he had on roller skates. He suddenly leaned back and flung the arm holding the flashlight into the air. The light glanced off the ceiling and the porch columns. He stepped his other foot to the side to get his balance.

"Something rolled under my feet." He stepped back and shined his light down onto the porch. Matthew and Nick tiptoed up to look. At Uncle Roy's feet were two arrows. They looked like they had been parallel until Uncle Roy stepped on them. They were facing opposite directions.

"Looks like you were right. Someone was here."

CHAPTER 9

FRIDAY MORNING, JUNE 20

Matthew tossed and turned for the rest of the night and got up the next morning feeling tired and uneasy. During breakfast no one mentioned what had occurred during the night, and since Mom and Kate were on the back side of the house, apparently, they had not heard anything.

Around nine o'clock Mom and Kate left in the SUV to go down to the Steward house for a cake-baking-and-icing lesson that Ms. Sarah had planned for Kate.

"Ms. Sarah has a pan shaped like a flower," Kate told them at breakfast. "She's going to show me how to decorate it."

"What kind of cake are you going to make?" asked Matthew.

"I don't know," said Kate in an off-handed way as if that didn't really matter.

"Matthew, I'm leaving you my phone," Mom said as she handed him the cell phone. "You can call Ms. Sarah's number if you need anything." She and Kate climbed into the SUV and rattled across the cattle guard onto the road.

They had not been gone long when Mr. Charlie showed up with Abby, who was walking up the steps as Uncle Roy went into the yard to talk with Mr. Charlie.

"You're not going to believe what happened last night," said Nick to Abby as she entered the living room.

"Wait. We need to hear what Uncle Roy and Mr. Charlie are talking about," said Matthew. He looked at Abby. "Do you know?" Abby shook her head.

Nick crept to the front door and cracked it open. "Shh,"

he said. "I'll try to listen." Matthew and Abby watched from the window.

About a minute later, Matthew saw his uncle turn and walk back toward the porch. "He's coming," Matthew warned. Nick quietly closed the door and quickly sat on the couch. The other two scrambled to the chair and piano bench.

"I'm going out with Charlie for a while," Uncle Roy said as he came into the house. "Should be back in an hour or two." He walked down the hall to his bedroom.

Mr. Charlie walked into the house behind Uncle Roy. He looked sternly at the three kids and said, "Y'all remember to stay out of the woods and not walk down to the house, ya hear? Roy said you have your mom's cell phone, Matt." Matthew nodded his head. "Call if you see anything unusual on the road."

All three nodded as Uncle Roy returned wearing his leather work boots instead of sneakers. As Uncle Roy's car followed Mr. Charlie's truck across the cattle guard, Matthew wondered why Uncle Roy didn't just ride with Mr. Charlie.

"Guys," Abby said, "what happened last night?"

Matthew and Nick told her about hearing someone on the porch and seeing the dark form go over the fence.

"I think it might be an Indian spirit," said Nick.

Matthew shook his head. "Don't think so, Nick."

"Maybe when Caddo Indian Cabin Man moved in, he woke up a spirit or something," said Nick.

"His name is Mr. Washington," Abby corrected.

Nick shrugged his shoulders.

"I think that's a little far-fetched," Matthew said although he did wonder about the feeling that someone was in the bedroom last night.

"That's not all, Abby," said Matthew. "Then Uncle Roy came onto the porch because he heard us. He found two arrows on the front porch . . . when he stepped on them."

"Wow," said Abby. "So someone actually came up to the house?"

"Well, if it was a person, they waited until all the lights were out," said Nick. "That doesn't sound too brave to me. It's not like it was the witching hour. It was only about 10:30."

"That kind of negates your Indian spirit theory," said Abby, gazing at Nick.

"Who says that Indians believe in that twelve midnight thing?" said Nick, shrugging his shoulders.

"Where on the porch were the arrows?" asked Abby, looking back at Matthew. The boys took her to the front porch to show her where the arrows had been lying, close to the porch steps.

"I guess we wouldn't have found them until morning if Nick and I hadn't been up looking for the light," said Matthew.

"What do you mean? What light?"

"After you left last night, I thought I saw a light in the woods."

"No kidding?!" said Abby.

"Which he didn't tell me about until we went to bed," said Nick, frowning at Matthew.

Matthew shrugged. "Well, anyway, we got up to look. That's when we heard someone on the porch."

"And found the arrows."

"They were laid parallel to each other, facing in opposite directions."

"Where are the arrows now?" said Abby, looking around the porch.

"I think Uncle Roy has them."

"I wish we could Google what the arrows mean, but Granddad told us specifically not to walk to the house."

"My mom left her phone here. We could use it." Matthew grabbed the phone from the top of the piano and clicked the internet icon. "Do you remember which website had all those symbols, Abby?"

She named what she thought it was and then said, "Type that in as a Google search. Even if that's not exactly right, the website should pop up as one of the choices."

"Good idea," said Nick.

The cell phone was slow to load the site. Abby and Nick crowded around Matthew, trying to see the small screen over his shoulders. Finally, the site loaded and Matthew began scrolling down, again having to wait for new sections of the screen to load.

"This is taking forever," said Nick.

"We have crappy cell phone service out here," said Matthew.

Finally they found the image, two arrows laid out parallel to each other but pointing in opposite directions. Matthew turned the phone lengthwise so that the words showed beside the image.

"Here we go," said Matthew. "This means 'war.'"

"Yeah, Matt, I like your attitude. Let's go get 'em," said Nick, pumping his arm.

"No, Nick," said Abby, taking the cell phone from Matthew and looking at the screen. "He means that the two arrows make a symbol that literally means that one tribe is declaring war on another."

All three just stood for a few seconds.

"So, the spirits want to attack us?" asked Nick.

"Not sure what it means, Nick," Matthew said slowly. "What did you hear Uncle Roy and Mr. Charlie saying outside?"

"Only a few words. I heard 'boat' and 'lake' and 'landing.' Then I heard your Uncle Roy say, 'Let's go.'" Nick plopped down on the living room sofa.

Matthew nodded. "What did your granddad mean about keeping our eyes on the road?" Matthew walked to the living room window and looked out.

"I don't know."

"Should we be watching for Mr. Washington?" asked Nick.

"I thought they didn't suspect him," said Matthew.

Abby was still standing in the middle of the room. After a moment, she said, "It sounds like they are taking Granddad's boat out on the lake."

The thought hit Matthew like a splash of cold lake water. He couldn't believe what he was hearing. He and Nick and Abby had done all the leg work. Now the adults were sidelining them and taking over.

"They tell us to stay put," Matthew said, turning from the window and walking in front of the chair. "Then they go out on the lake without us like we didn't help at all."

"I don't think they are just going fishin'," said Nick.

"Why shouldn't we go?" said Matthew, his voice rising. "We gave them most of the information."

"Yeah, we did," said Nick, standing up from the couch.

"We suspected that whoever is going into the woods is getting there from the lake," said Matthew.

"Yeah," said Abby. "They would kinda have to. The only people we have seen driving down this road live on it."

"Which supports my spirit theory," said Nick. The other two turned to glare at him, Abby with her hands on her hips.

"Just saying," said Nick, returning to his seat on the couch.

"But the lake is really shallow in this inlet," said Matthew. "That's why we don't usually go swimming here. Too mucky. Anything bigger than an aluminum fishing boat has a hard time navigating this far up," Matthew said as he sat down on the edge of the chair.

"Wouldn't we have heard the motor if they came past the house?" asked Nick.

"What if they weren't using the motor? When Granddad takes me out in his fishing boat, we don't use the motor in the inlet. We paddle." Abby walked over to the piano bench and sat down, sticking her sneaker-clad feet out in front of her.

"That's how someone got into the woods without us seeing them. If they came up the inlet by paddling their boat, we wouldn't hear anything."

"So we wouldn't have looked," added Nick.

"It would help if we could see the woods from the lake," said Abby.

"Maybe that's what your Uncle Roy and Mr. Charlie are doing," said Nick.

Matthew jumped up. "Hey, I think Uncle Roy left his canoe here. It's stored in the carport." Matthew dashed out the front door and down the porch steps. Nick and Abby ran after him. They all sprinted to the back corner of the yard where the open carport sat against the fence line.

Matthew looked up into the open rafter area as he entered the building. "There it is, up there." He grabbed an old milk crate from where it sat against the wall, flipped it over, and dragged it under the canoe. "Help me get this thing down."

"Yeah, Abby, help us." Nick grabbed another crate, turned it over, and stepped onto it beside Matthew.

"I don't know if this is such a good idea, guys. What if Granddad sees us?" said Abby.

Matthew and Nick were already working the canoe out of the ropes holding it to the rafters. It started to fall as they pushed together at one end, so Abby grabbed the other end. A moment later they had it on the ground.

"He didn't tell us not to go on the lake," Matthew said as he turned to look at Abby.

"He told us to stay out of the woods and off the road," said Nick.

Abby shrugged her shoulders and looked at the canoe.

"Look around. Do you see the paddles?" asked Matthew.

"I don't see any," said Nick, looking behind an old barrel.

"Wait, I think I saw them in the shed." Matthew ran around to the tool shed door.

"Matt!" Abby called after him. "Are you sure this thing will be okay to put in the lake?"

"Why not?" asked Nick.

Nick was pulling the canoe out of the carport as Matthew

emerged from the tool shed with two wooden paddles. "I'm going. Are you coming?" he asked Abby.

Abby hesitated, then said, "Well, you're not going without me."

She grabbed the paddles as the boys each picked up an end of the canoe. They started across the lawn behind the house.

Matthew suddenly put down his end of the canoe and headed for the screened door on the back porch.

"Where're you going?" asked Abby.

"Be right back," he said as the screen door slammed.

A moment later, Matthew came out the door wearing rubber boots.

Nick nodded approvingly. "I wish you had a pair for me."

"When's the last time you used this canoe?" asked Abby, heading down the hill toward the lake.

"Last summer." Matthew picked up the canoe again.

"Where exactly are we going?" she asked.

"I don't know. I guess far enough into the inlet to see what the shore looks like from the lake."

"We should check out the woods down past your house—you know, where the fire was—as well as the opposite side where someone shot at Mr. Steward," said Nick as he struggled down the hill with the back end of the canoe.

"I'm surprised that you haven't come up with a name for our mystery person," said Matthew.

"I'll think on it," Nick said, smiling.

"I guess we should check for places where a boat would have scraped the ground when someone pulled it up on shore," said Abby.

"You're finally *on board* with me?" said Matthew as they reached the lake.

Abby laughed. "Nice pun. I guess I was nervous about Granddad being shot at and then y'all finding the two arrows last night. But we haven't gotten this far in our investigation to stop now."

"You're right, Abby. You are good at this," said Matthew. "We all are!" said Nick.

As they approached the lake, they angled for the far side of the dock and put the canoe in the water. Abby and Nick climbed in, and Matthew waded into the water to push the canoe farther into the lake. He carefully climbed aboard so as not to tilt it over.

The canoe floated into the middle of the inlet with Matthew and Nick paddling. Abby kneeled on the floor of the canoe between the two seats.

Abby looked back at the shoreline. "Hey, guys, go to the left. Can we see the mound from the lake?"

"Boy Scout camp is coming in handy," said Nick as he switched his paddle to the right side of the canoe to turn it.

Matthew looked up to get his bearings and noticed the hawk.

It flew over the water from the dock toward the trees on the opposite side of the inlet. As he followed its path, he noticed the flash of an aluminum fishing boat heading toward them from farther up the inlet. Paddling it was the dark-haired man—the one they had seen in the green truck.

"Uh oh," said Abby. "We got a problem." She lifted her hand and looked at the water dripping from it.

"What?" asked Nick.

"I thought you said you used this boat last summer. Did it leak then? I've got water around my knees."

"Yep. It's getting on my shoes," said Nick, looking down from his paddling to the puddle of water around his sneakers.

"We got more trouble than that. Look." Matthew nodded his head toward the approaching boat.

"Who's that?" asked Abby.

"Is that Mr. Washington?" said Nick.

"Nick, we need to aim for those trees over there." Matthew pointed to the cypress grove that grew in the water across the inlet from the dock. "Maybe he hasn't seen us yet."

As water continued to leak in, Matthew and Nick paddled like madmen to get the canoe in the trees before it sank. Abby used her cupped hands to scoop water over the side.

"Matt, hand me the paddle and get ready to jump out to pull us in," said Abby.

"Abby," said Matthew, looking around, "there's not really a shore here. It's a swampy area with trees right in the lake."

"Then we need to go a different way. We're about to sink!" said Abby. About that time the edge of the canoe hit a cypress knee sticking out of the water and more water rushed in.

"Too late for that," said Nick. "And besides there are only trees everywhere you look."

They maneuvered the canoe between the cypress knees and the stand of three close trees. A crow squawked at them from the branches above their heads.

"Then we better grab onto the trees. The water is coming in faster than I can get it out," said Abby. With water covering their feet, they all started scooping water with their cupped hands.

"Maybe if I take off my shoe and scoop with that—" Nick suddenly gasped. He glanced over at the hand that was lying on his shoulder. Matthew and Abby looked up with wide eyes. Mr. Washington's aluminum fishing boat was beside their canoe, and Mr. Washington's hand was on Nick's shoulder.

Abby and Matthew lunged toward Nick, but the dark-haired man held up his hand for them to stop. Then he put his finger to his lips for them to be silent. The quiet sternness in his face stopped them.

He motioned for them to get into his boat.

Matthew started to protest, but they didn't really have a choice as the canoe continued to fill with water. Nick, Abby, and Matthew scrambled into Mr. Washington's boat.

Mr. Washington guided his boat further into the cypress trees.

Nick took off his sodden sneaker and emptied the water over the edge of the boat. "Well, sir, you got us now. What you gonna do with us?"

"I guess I'm stuck with you for the moment," Mr. Washington said in a low voice, almost a whisper. "Look." He pointed to the area of the inlet that opened into the lake. Another aluminum boat was entering, but it wasn't Mr. Charlie's boat. "I need to watch what this couple does."

The outboard motor was off and angled out of the water. A man and a woman were paddling down the middle of the inlet.

In a whisper Matthew sputtered, "I know her! She came by the house last week."

"Yes," said Mr. Washington, "and I need to see what they're doing now. Y'all have to be quiet and watch." He looked at Nick for his cooperation. Nick nodded.

Mr. Washington reached under his seat, pulled out a camera, and started taking pictures. Matthew noticed the telephoto lens. The woman, whom Matthew remembered was named Heather, and the man paddled past the Morin house and then angled their boat toward the shore in the area that led up to the mound. The man hopped out to pull the boat ashore.

Mr. Washington kept taking pictures. Matthew, Abby, and Nick didn't take their eyes off the pair as they pulled shovels, an orange bucket, and a rifle out of the bottom of the boat and began to climb the ridge.

With quiet anguish, Nick said, "Sir, we have to stop them."

"Not yet," was all Mr. Washington said.

"But they are going to dig up the mound!"

"Shh," Mr. Washington said. He turned and reached behind his seat for a radio that looked like the one that Deputy Ramsey had carried.

Mr. Washington clicked on the side button and quietly said, "They're here, Doug. Headin' up the ridge."

"Copy that," was the answer.

Then they just sat in the boat in the cover of the trees. The waiting was almost too much for the three kids. Abby bit her fingernails. Nick leaned over the edge of the boat, trying to get a better look. Matthew mentally clicked back through their evidence.

He had completely overlooked Heather and her pushy visit the second day they had been at the house. She said her company wanted to buy their land. Now Matthew doubted that was her real motive.

The radio clicked. A voice said, "We see them. Be ready, Herb."

"Copy that," answered Mr. Washington as he gave the three a serious look. "We need to stop this pair and their thieving ways, and I don't want to miss this chance. I don't know how desperate they are or what they will try. And I wasn't counting on you being here. This is going to be risky with you along. You must *absolutely* do *exactly* what I say. No argument. Okay?"

"Yes, sir," all three answered.

"I'm sorry for suspecting you, sir," Nick said.

Mr. Washington smiled and whispered, "We'll talk later." He put down his camera and reached behind his seat again. He pulled out a rifle.

"Whoa," Nick said. Mr. Washington again put his finger to his lips again. Nick hunkered down in the boat.

"You two get down, too," Mr. Washington told Abby and Matthew. "And stay down, no matter what."

Abby, the smallest of the three, climbed over the front seat and scrunched down in the bow. Nick and Matthew squeezed into the area between two seats. Mr. Washington sat in the back.

He paddled his boat forward but not toward the other boat. He turned north toward the main part of the lake, staying in the trees as much as possible. Nick rose up a little to look over the edge of the boat toward the mound area, but Mr. Washington pushed his head down with a paddle.

At the northern-most area of the tree cover, Mr. Washington grabbed a tree to stop the boat. There they waited.

A moment later, the radio crackled again. "They're running, Herb. Should be coming your way before long."

Matthew wanted to look so badly. The man and woman must be running for their boat. Someone, probably the deputies, must be in the woods chasing them.

The boat drifted. As they cleared the trees, Matthew heard the other boat's motor start. Then Mr. Washington also started his motor.

Nick said, "They're trying to get away!"

The other boat's motor surged. The sound seemed to be in front of their boat, and suddenly Mr. Washington's boat also charged forward. Matthew noticed that they were no longer in the protection of the cypress trees. The radio button clicked and Matthew heard Mr. Washington say, "They're heading east, Doug."

A rifle shot sounded. Matthew and Nick both flinched. Matthew thought he heard a screech from Abby. He tried to look up to see, but their boat swung suddenly to the left, and he was pushed against Nick. Mr. Washington said again, "Stay down."

Matthew couldn't believe this was happening. Someone in the other boat must have shot at them!

That warning from Mr. Washington wasn't necessary anymore. Matthew didn't lift his head again!

Spray came over the sides of the boat as Mr. Washington cranked up the engine and swung the boat back. Matthew held tight to the seat in front of him as the boat lunged over the rough surface of the wake from the other boat.

Matthew heard the other boat's motor on the right side of their boat and felt their boat veer to the right. He knew they were close to docks of other houses in this area of the lake.

They swung suddenly to the left and back to the right. Matthew heard a voice holler, "Hey, watch it!" He figured that they had gotten too close to a dock where someone was standing.

They felt a thump and heard a scraping sound on the bottom of their boat and suddenly they were airborne. All three kids rose off the bottom of the boat. They came back down with the loud thwack of the boat on the water's surface. "We must have hit a stump or something," said Nick above the roar of the boat's motor. Matthew thought of the sinking canoe and looked as far around as he could at the bottom of the boat. No water yet. He glanced at Mr. Washington. His hand was on the throttle of the motor, his mouth was a thin line, and he was looking forward with a determined look.

Again Mr. Washington angled their boat to the left and then to the right. Matthew wanted to see how close they had come to a dock but kept his head down, that rifle shot still ringing in his ears.

The motor from the other boat suddenly sounded different although he couldn't tell why. He felt their boat swing abruptly to the far left, squeezing Matthew against Nick again. A spray of water splashed Matthew as he heard a boat zoom by them from the opposite direction. Was that the suspects' boat? What were they doing? It didn't make sense that they would go back the other way.

"What's going on?" asked Nick.

"I can't tell," said Matthew. "I think they just came back toward us."

The roaring of the motor changed again, and the other boat was now on the far side of Mr. Washington's boat, not behind it. The suspects must have circled around and their boat was now going the same way. What were they doing? How was this helping them get away? The sounds from both motors roared and echoed. They must be under the highway bridge. Mr. Washington swung his boat to the right, away from the sound of the other boat.

Matthew felt a strong jolt, the boat lunged to the right,

and, once again, the boat was airborne. All three kids flew off the bottom of the boat again. Mr. Washington's boat rammed into one of the concrete abutments of the bridge. Abby screamed. Matthew looked her way just in time to see her fly out the left side of the boat. The suspects' boat was already past them and was speeding out from under the bridge.

Mr. Washington immediately let off the throttle and began circling the boat back. "Can she swim?" he asked.

"I don't know," Matthew yelled back. He got on the boat seat and looked around in the water to find Abby. Mr. Washington was handing Nick a life jacket from the back of the boat.

Then Mr. Washington clicked the radio button. "They're heading toward Smith's Landing, Doug. I'm easing up."

"Copy that," came the voice through the radio.

The waves from the other boat made the water rough between the bridge abutments. The boat was bobbing in the waves. Matthew searched the water on the right side of the boat.

"I don't see her," yelled Nick. "Could we be on top of her?" Nick was leaning over the left side, looking into the lake.

"I don't think so," said Mr. Washington, but he was leaning over the side of the boat, looking behind.

"Could the other boat have hit her?" asked Matthew, looking back at Mr. Washington.

"I think they were past us when she flew out."

Matthew scanned the water between the boat and the bridge abutment. Mr. Charlie and Ms. Sarah were going to kill them. This was awful. What if she was hurt in the water? Then he saw her head break the surface of the water between the boat and the bridge support. "There she is," he yelled, pointing at Abby, but she was facing away from the boat and didn't see them. She started to swim toward the abutment.

"Abby," Matthew yelled with his hands cupped around his mouth. She kept swimming. "Yell with me," Matthew said to Nick. They yelled her name together. She looked their way and waved. Mr. Washington turned the boat and eased the throttle forward, pulling up beside where Abby was floating. Nick leaned over with the life jacket, but Abby didn't put it on. She merely clutched it under her left arm and lifted her right hand toward Matthew and Nick. They grabbed her and pulled her onto the boat.

Abby sat on the front seat and tried to wring the water out of her long hair. Matthew watched as she felt for a scrunchie to pull it back, but it was gone. A shirt came over his shoulder and he looked back. Mr. Washington had on just his white tee shirt. Matthew helped Abby drape the shirt over her shoulders.

"Are you okay?" said Mr. Washington. Abby just nodded. She shivered a little, but then her shoulders seemed to relax some.

Mr. Washington steered his boat through the concrete supports of the bridge, and the boat surged into the open area again. Matthew saw the suspects' boat speeding across the lake.

Matthew could hear another motor—a much deeper sound from a larger motor. With no need to huddle in the bottom of the boat now, Matthew saw the larger boat coming from the right.

Matthew heard another rifle report and then an amplified voice that said, "This is the Caddo Parish Sheriff's Marine Unit. Shut off your boat motor and lower your weapon."

Matthew felt Mr. Washington ease off the throttle. He heard another rifle shot, but a glance at Mr. Washington showed that he was not concerned.

Matthew heard the second warning from the sheriff's boat. He could see the suspects' boat still trying to get away. Nick turned to him and said, "They must be stupid if they think they can outrun that sheriff boat."

Matthew heard the deep sound of a fourth engine coming from under the bridge. It was definitely not a fishing boat. He saw another sheriff's marine unit approaching.

Mr. Washington let their boat drift where it was. They could see all the boats in front of them. The sheriff's units were approaching the suspects' boat from both sides.

The motor of the small boat stopped. Matthew could hear lots of yelling about putting down weapons and putting hands up.

"Boy, I wish I was closer," said Nick. All three kids leaned forward in the boat.

"Don't tump us over," Mr. Washington warned. He sounded relaxed although his hand was still on the rifle across his knees.

What the three kids saw looked like a scene from an action movie. The sheriff's deputies from the two marine units were standing on their boats pointing rifles down on the suspects in their boat. The man and woman were huddled in the bottom of their boat as a sheriff's deputy climbed over the side and stepped onto their boat. He picked up the suspects' rifle and handed it to someone on the sheriff's boat to the left. He handcuffed the man and pulled him into a standing position. The deputy passed him to a deputy on the bigger boat. Then he passed a rope to the same deputy to tie off the smaller boat.

Matthew saw the deputies putting the man face down on the deck on the sheriff's boat. Then the same procedure was carried out on the woman, who was handed over to the sheriff's boat on the right.

The deputy with the rifle in the small boat handed his firearm to another deputy on the sheriff's boat before climbing onto it.

"Did you see that?" said Nick. "That was good gun safety. You should take that firearm safety class I took, Matt. It was really cool."

Matthew nodded to Nick. Abby never took her eyes off

the scene in front of her. The sheriff's boats started forward with the suspects' boat in tow. Mr. Washington urged his boat forward, too.

"Are we going to follow them?" asked Nick excitedly, turning to look at Mr. Washington.

"Deputy Ramsey is waiting for me at the dock," said Mr. Washington, "so we have to go that way. He needs these pictures." He paused and smiled slightly. "Y'all gave me quite a start when I saw you in the inlet with a sinking canoe."

"Kinda scared us too," said Nick.

"I knew that thieving pair was coming, and I was concerned that they would see you."

"I'm glad they didn't get away."

"And that we didn't sink," said Abby.

"I think there might be someone who will want to see you at the boat launch."

"Granddad is there?"

"Yeah."

"Uh oh," said Nick, looking at Matthew.

Matthew shrugged his shoulders. "Time to face the music."

The launch area of Smith's Landing flashed with the blue and red lights of several sheriff's cars in the parking lot. The sheriff's boats eased up to the dock. The two prisoners were handed over to the waiting deputies.

Then Matthew spied Mr. Charlie and Uncle Roy standing beside Mr. Charlie's blue truck. Mr. Washington tied his boat to the dock and told the kids they could get out.

Matthew's knees were a little shaky on the wooden planks of the dock as he climbed out of the boat. Nick and Abby climbed out slowly too. Matthew almost stepped back into the boat when he saw Mr. Charlie and Uncle Roy walking toward them with surprised looks on their faces. Nick and Abby were watching the adults too. Matthew wondered what the adults would say—and do—to them since, technically, they didn't exactly follow their instructions and they almost lost Abby. That swaying boat race, while exciting, now seemed a little scary.

Mr. Washington approached the two men, introduced himself, and shook hands. "Sorry I haven't taken an opportunity to introduce myself properly before now."

"Abby, what happened?" Mr. Charlie said. Abby walked over to her granddad who put his arm around her shoulders. She shivered a little.

"The kids are fine although probably a little shaken up and," said Mr. Washington, looking at Abby, "maybe a little wet. I think they have quite a story to tell you."

"It looks like it," said Uncle Roy.

Matthew's stomach felt a little queasy and Nick and Abby both looked a little pale.

Uncle Roy turned to Mr. Charlie and said, "Charlie, does that bait shop have cokes? You kids want something to drink?"

"Yes, sir," said Matthew with Abby and Nick nodding in agreement.

"I need to check my boat. Y'all excuse me." Mr. Washington turned and walked back to his boat.

Over soft drinks at a wooden picnic table by the dock, the three kids gave a short version of the other boat coming into the inlet and the man and woman going up the ridge to the mound. They also told how Mr. Washington took pictures and chased the other boat out of the inlet.

As they warmed to their story, the three kids grew so excited that the two men had to keep reminding them not to all talk at once. From the boat launch area the men had viewed the sheriff's units apprehending the pair of suspects so they knew that part of the story, but they looked at Abby with concern when they heard about her flight into the water.

"Abby, you could have been hurt!" Mr. Charlie said.

"I'm fine, Granddad, but I would like to get some dry clothes."

"Give me a minute and then we'll go," said Mr. Charlie.

The men went to talk to Mr. Washington and Deputy Ramsey as the three kids finished their colas.

"Who was that lady in the boat, Matt? You said that you had seen her before," said Abby.

"I don't know why I didn't think of her before," said Matthew. "She came by the house early last week. She said her company wanted to buy our land."

"Why?" asked Abby, pulling Mr. Washington's shirt a little closer around her.

"Actually, she didn't say."

"Well, I think we know *now!*" said Nick. "They wanted to dig up that Indian mound!"

"I'm pretty sure I saw them in that boat the first day we were here. I thought they were fishing," said Matthew.

"They must have been scouting out the area," said Nick.

"I bet they already knew what they were looking for," said Abby. "They were probably not happy to see your family at the house."

"Oh, the bucket. I need to ask Mr. Charlie about the orange bucket," said Matthew. Abby and Nick looked at him with questioning eyes, but Matthew was watching Uncle Roy, Mr. Charlie, and Mr. Washington walk toward them.

"Let's go back to the house," said Mr. Charlie before Matthew could say anything about the bucket. "The ladies will be worried about us."

"Oh, no!" Matthew said suddenly. "Uncle Roy, Mom doesn't know where we are. If she goes back to the house . . ."

"I called her, Matt. She is expecting an explanation when we get back. I think we all need to hear more of this story," said Uncle Roy.

Matthew, Abby, and Nick looked at each other. They were going to be in trouble now.

"How are the boys going to get home, Granddad?" asked Abby. "We won't all fit in the cab of your truck."

"Is your car here, Uncle Roy?" asked Matthew.

"No. I left it at Charlie's," said Uncle Roy.

"If you haven't had too much boat-ridin' for today, Mr. Washington said he'd take you back across the lake. Are you okay with that?" said Mr. Charlie.

"Yeah," the boys answered together.

The ride from the boat launch back to the dock at the Morin house took only a few minutes, but it was time enough to talk to Mr. Washington over the low rumble of the boat motor. He explained that he had recently retired and expected to relax at the lake and fix up the house.

"Even before the fire, I had noticed some strange activity on the lake and in the woods. Later I saw all of you in the woods."

"Was that you that Abby saw through the trees when we were at the mound?" asked Matthew.

"It was," said Mr. Washington. "I suspected what might be going on and was keeping a watch out for that pair we caught. But I didn't want to alarm you."

"So you knew about the mound?" asked Nick.

"I knew a family story about one in the area, but no one remembered exactly where it was. When I checked out the woods after the fire, I saw it."

"So, how did you get involved with the sheriff's office?" asked Matthew.

"When Deputy Ramsey came to ask me about the problems you were having, I mentioned the mound. He said that you had found it also. One thing led to another and I volunteered to help. I must say I am impressed that you understood what that mound was."

Nick beamed proudly.

"I knew then that my suspicions were correct—that someone wanted to dig into the mound. When we thought that they would come back today, Deputy Ramsey asked me to watch this end of the inlet."

"Kind of like a stake out! I guess you have experience, being a wildlife agent," said Nick.

"That's right," Mr. Washington said. "I must say, it was fun. Retirement can get boring."

Mr. Washington cut the motor as the boat entered the inlet, and Matthew helped him paddle toward the dock. "This has been a good morning's work, and I'm hungry. I'm planning on having rattlesnake steak for lunch. Want to join me?"

"I think we'll pass, Mr. Washington," said Matthew. "My mom is expecting us."

The boys climbed out of the boat onto the dock.

"Maybe some other time," said Nick. "I wouldn't mind trying it."

They waved as Mr. Washington paddled down the inlet toward his dock.

Walking up the hill to the house, Nick said, "So that's why we saw him with that snake skin."

"Yeah, we got that part wrong, but we got most of it right," said Matthew. The two high-fived each other.

"Now, we need to know why Uncle Roy and Mr. Charlie were already at the boat launch when we got there."

Mom stood at the kitchen door with her hands on her hips and a stern look on her face as they came up the hill from the lake. Ms. Sarah was standing behind her.

"Are you kids crazy? You could have gotten killed!" Mom said.

"My Lord, what did you children think you were doing?" said Ms. Sarah.

Kate was staring at them. "You got shot at?" she said.

"Not really. We were hunkered down in Mr. Washington's boat," said Matthew, although he knew he was simplifying what had happened. "Mom, did y'all bring that cake down here? I'm starving."

"That cake is our dessert tonight," said Kate in her best grown-up voice. "You can't have any 'til then."

Matthew and Nick climbed the back porch stairs and they all went into the house.

"I could wring your necks," Mom said, looking at the boys.

"We're fine, Mom. But hungry," Matthew said.

"How about sandwiches? It's almost lunch time." Mom and Ms. Sarah began pulling out the ham and fixings, and they all headed for the dining room.

Sandwiches made, Ms. Sarah said, "How exactly did y'all end up in Mr. Washington's boat?"

"Our canoe was sinking," said Matthew, munching a chip.

"And he saved us," Nick said, between bites of his sandwich.

"Canoe?" said Mom. "Matthew, you got that old canoe out of the carport? That thing has a slit in one of the seams."

"Yeah, we found that out," said Matthew, reaching for more chips.

"Yeah. Then he had to chase that other boat," said Nick.

"I can't believe you did this. Didn't Mr. Charlie tell you to stay in the house?" said Mom.

"Actually, he told us not to go in the woods or walk to his house. He didn't say anything about the lake." Matthew knew he was taking a chance.

Mom just stared at him. Then she shook her head.

He and Nick explained that they took the canoe out to see if someone had been coming to the mound from the lake. "Then everything started happening at once," said Matthew, reaching for a carrot stick.

Nick swallowed a bite of sandwich and added, "This other boat came into the inlet. They headed for the shore by the ridge."

"Mom, the lady in the boat was that same one who came here the day we were painting the porch. Remember, she said her name was Heather?"

"I remember, Matthew." She sighed and rubbed her hand across her eyes. Ms. Sarah patted her on the back.

"She said they wanted to buy our land, but that was obviously not what she was after."

"Those people were trying to steal artifacts out of the mound," said Abby as she walked into the dining room; she had on dry clothes.

"That's right, Abby," said Uncle Roy as he and Mr. Charlie entered behind her.

"But how did y'all know they were coming today?" asked Matthew.

"And where were you and Granddad going when you left here this morning?" said Abby.

"And where is my canoe?" said Uncle Roy with a twinkle in his eye.

Later that afternoon, Matthew saw the hawk sitting on the power line as he, Abby, and Nick walked down the road to Mr. Washington's cabin.

Uncle Roy, tied up with the sheriff's department all afternoon, had promised to answer all their questions that night. The three were sent to ask Mr. Washington to join everyone at the Stewards' for dinner.

Sheriff and state police cars were parked along the road while detectives searched the area around the mound and by the lake. Deputy Ramsey had even interviewed Matthew, Abby, and Nick.

Staring at the pine trees past the police cars, Nick said, "This has been the best week I've ever had. I'm almost looking forward to writing that 'What did you do during your summer vacation?' essay when we get back to school."

"I wish we could see what they're doing in the woods," said Matthew, also staring into the pine woods.

"Yeah, the rest of the summer at home will be dull after this," said Abby.

"When are you going home?" said Matthew.

"My parents are coming tomorrow. We'll leave on Sunday."

"Matt's mom is probably taking me back to Shreveport tomorrow," said Nick. "I think my parents are upset about what's happened."

"They know about this?" asked Abby.

"Yeah. Matt's mom called them. I thought my mom was going to come and get me right then, but we convinced her that there was no danger . . . anymore," he said with a smile.

They were approaching the cabin as Mr. Washington walked into his yard from the woods. He waved and walked their way. "What're you kids doing down here?"

"Grandma sent us to invite you to dinner at our house tonight," Abby said. "Can you come?"

"I'd be pleased to. What time?"

They told him and then Matthew said, "Mr. Washington, how did y'all know those people would come back today? All Uncle Roy said was that he'd explain later."

"You three really had an adventure today, and I know that you have questions. But can you wait till tonight?"

The three reluctantly nodded their heads.

CHAPTER 10

FRIDAY EVENING, JUNE 20

Matthew and the others devoured Ms. Sarah's dinner of meat loaf and mashed potatoes that night. After dinner, Kate—with a huge grin on her face—brought the flower-shaped cake decorated with pink and blue icing to the table.

Carrying cake slices and refilled glasses of iced tea, the group settled on the back porch. The adults were in the porch furniture and the kids scattered themselves on the floor and the steps.

Uncle Roy took a big bite of cake and, looking at Kate, said, "Yum! I wonder what talented young lady made this cake?"

"I did," said Kate, smiling at him. She had a little blue icing from the cake on her lips.

"It sure is good," said Mr. Washington, taking a big bite. The others around the porch nodded in agreement.

Matthew put down his empty plate and leaned toward Uncle Roy. "So, Uncle Roy, will you tell us now? Please. How'd y'all know those people were coming back today?"

"We didn't for sure, but we knew that they have been in the woods several times," Uncle Roy said.

"That's right," said Mr. Washington. "I observed them both on the lake and in the woods. I think that they were trying to avoid being seen by you and your family, but they weren't as careful as they thought."

"So, it was Heather and that man?" asked Matthew.

"That's right," said Mr. Washington. "They call themselves Jonson Land Enterprises."

"That's what was on her business card," said Matthew. Mom nodded her agreement. "They were trying to scare us off, weren't they?"

"Yep, they were," said Mr. Charlie. "That's why they shot above my head. They were hopin' you would tuck tail and run, and I wouldn't snoop in the woods."

"So what was different about today?" asked Abby, wrapping her arms around her knees.

"We set them up," said Mr. Charlie, picking up his tea glass.

"We knew that they had been watching your house, hoping you would leave. We decided to let them think you had," said Mr. Washington.

"But the house was empty when we went home last weekend. Couldn't they have dug up the mound then?" asked Matthew.

"You would think so," said Uncle Roy. "Maybe they were at another site, or maybe that spot was just too 'hot,' excuse the pun, for them to go back so soon after the fire."

"They seem to be opportunists," said Mom. "When they found your pine straw and logs in the woods, they set it on fire." Mom put her plate on the table as Kate scooted over closer to her on the wicker loveseat.

"We also had a plan," said Mr. Charlie as he rocked in his chair. "Roy and I, supposedly, went out on the lake to go fishin'. Kate and your mom came up here to bake. All the cars were gone. That left only you three at the house, but they wouldn't know that."

"Now that I think about it," Matthew said as he looked at Mom, "I'm surprised about that. You wouldn't let us stay by ourselves back at our house, but you left the three of us alone here?"

Mom put her arm around Kate and said, "Roy convinced me. We felt that you three would be fine if you stayed at the house. I thought y'all would play video games. And it was also a way to keep you out of the action, so to speak. I left you my cell phone, just in case."

"Y'all had impressed me with all you had done and figured out so far," said Uncle Roy. "You seemed very mature in your thinking."

"Thanks," said Nick, sitting up, puffing out his chest, and smiling broadly from where he leaned against a porch pillar. Everyone laughed.

"So what was the plan?" asked Matthew. "Which you left us out of, by the way."

Uncle Roy nodded at his comment. "I know we did, Matt, but we didn't have a choice. It's not like the sheriff's office was going to let you help."

"I guess not."

"So the plan was to make the Jonsons think we were gone for the day. No cars there and so on," said Uncle Roy. "We were confident that all they wanted was to dig up the mound. We were all keeping watch."

"And I told you to keep a watch on the road in case they drove in," said Mr. Charlie.

Matthew nodded. "But we didn't exactly stay put, did we?"

"Thank goodness Mr. Washington was there to keep you from sinking into the lake," said Mom. "I don't know what I would have done if something had happened to you—well, any of you." Kate had fallen asleep and Mom lay Kate's head down on her lap.

"Uh, is there any more cake?" Nick smiled sheepishly, holding out his plate.

"Me, too," said Matt, hopping up with his plate.

"I'll get it," said Ms. Sarah. "I don't suppose y'all want to miss any of this story." Nick nodded and smiled. Taking their plates, Ms. Sarah disappeared into the kitchen.

"So these mound robbers thought the coast was clear?" asked Nick.

"Something like that," said Uncle Roy.

"What about the sheriff's boats?" asked Abby.

"Why did the sheriff think that today was a good day?" asked Matthew.

"For a stakeout," added Nick.

"Remember when I told you that Deputy Ramsey looked really thoughtful when I told him about the possible mound?" said Uncle Roy. "It turns out that he knew about a desecrated historical site in a nearby parish. He talked to a colleague who investigates historical artifact crimes and learned that a group was searching for and digging up these sites in order to sell the artifacts."

"Like on the black market?" said Nick. Uncle Roy smiled and nodded.

"This is not the first time these people have desecrated Indian land," said Mr. Washington.

"After we alerted the sheriff's office to the mound's location here, the task force has been keeping an eye on these people's activities," said Uncle Roy.

"The Jonsons were running out of time to sell any artifacts because their buyer was getting skittish, according to a criminal informant," said Mr. Washington.

"Wow! The sheriff has CIs, like someone on the inside reporting their activities?" asked Nick.

Uncle Roy nodded and said, "Not necessarily what they did, but actions related to the selling of artifacts."

"That's so cool," said Abby.

"Like in a movie," said Nick.

"How did the robbers know the mound was there?" asked Abby.

"They do a lot of research," Mr. Washington said. "They read books about local history and investigate possible sites. They know what to look for. The one named Heather has an archeology degree."

"She could do a lot of good if she worked for the state to find architectural artifacts, but they chose to be in the business of selling artifacts illegally," said Mom. "That made me really angry when I found that out."

"And they are smart enough to keep changing the name of the company. Their name isn't really Jonson. That's one of their aliases," added Uncle Roy.

"Plus, the police have security video footage of them goin' into the historical museum in the old train station in town. It has an exhibit of hundreds of old photographs from area residents," said Mr. Charlie.

Ms. Sarah, returning with the slices of cake, added, "The photos show the community of the northern end of Caddo Parish." She handed the plates to the boys and settled into her rocking chair. "I helped sort and mount pictures for that project last year. Matt, one of those pictures shows your great-great-granddad and a 'Mr. Washington' standing in front of a small hill."

The three looked at Mr. Washington.

"Yes," he said. "That's probably my great-grandpa and the same mound."

"We saw that picture," said Nick, trying to talk around his bite of cake.

"In that old album Mom found in the attic," added Matthew.

"Was it that old leather-covered album with an M embossed on the cover?" Uncle Roy asked.

Mom nodded.

"I haven't seen that old album in years. Where'd you find it?"

"Kate wanted to see what was in the attic, and I was trying to keep her busy." She looked down and moved a blonde curl out of Kate's face. "I found the album in an old trunk under a box of arrowheads."

"You found the arrowheads?" asked Matthew, looking from Mom to Uncle Roy.

"Yes, but I was more interested in the photographs. I left the arrowheads in the attic."

"It's like someone wanted you to find it," said Abby.

"Indian spirits," said Nick.

"I wouldn't think so, Nick," said Mr. Washington. "All those stories about haunted Indian burial grounds are just that— stories. I guess they make good bonfire tales, but I've never heard one told by an Indian."

"Mr. Washington, what about Indian symbols? Do you know much about those?" asked Abby.

"Like what?"

"Tell him what we saw in the dirt, Matt," said Nick.

Matthew explained to the group about the drawing they had found in the dirt beside the burned logs. "It was a circle containing a woman and two children. The people were upside-down."

"Matthew, you didn't tell me about that drawing!" said Mom, with a surprised tone, her face showing her concern.

"I'm sorry, Mom." He looked down. "I didn't want you to worry."

"Is there anything else you haven't told me?"

"No, I don't think so," Matthew said, looking up at her. "I have to admit, I guess, that I didn't want you to pack us up and take us home. I was really mad that someone was trying to scare us. I tried to think what Dad would do."

Mom's eyes shone with unshed tears. Ms. Sarah patted her on the arm. "Matthew, you are becoming a mystery to me."

"They do that at this age," said Uncle Roy, smiling at her.

"Mr. Washington," said Matthew, "does that drawing have any meaning for you?"

"And don't forget the two arrows on the porch," said Nick.

"Our research showed that they both have to do with declaring war," said Abby.

"Doesn't sound like anything in Caddo Indian lore. The Caddo were not a warring nation, by nature."

"We read that too. You know," said Abby, with a knowing look, "those people could have found those symbols on the same website where we found them."

"Yeah. And make us think that an Indian was involved," said Nick.

"I guess they were trying to frighten you by implicating me in an underhanded way. They knew I lived down the road. The one named Heather came by my place also," said Mr. Washington.

"Yeah, I saw her turn down your way when she left our house," said Matthew.

"Well, we did suspect you for a while," Nick said to Mr. Washington. "Sorry about that again, sir."

Mr. Washington smiled and nodded to Nick.

"Deputy Ramsey told me that they would not have finalized the deal on the property. They only wanted access to the land," said Uncle Roy.

"So Heather and this man were trying to dig in the mound for artifacts," said Abby. "Why were they in the woods across from Granddad's house then?"

"Fresh bodies of water, like the stream, are another source for artifacts. That takes a lot more searching and digging," said Mr. Washington. "The original town was probably closer to the stream rather than the lake. It might have even been right where your house is now."

"Right where our house is? Cool," said Matthew. Then he paused and looked at Mr. Charlie. "Mr. Charlie, I forgot to ask you something. Did you leave an orange bucket in our yard?"

Mr. Charlie shook his head. "No, I don't have an orange one."

"I figured that," said Matthew. "I found it in the yard when we arrived. I think these people cut across the yard some time before we got here last week. They must have put the bucket down and accidentally left it there."

"Oh, they had a bucket like that with them today!" said Abby.

"That's probably something you need to show the task force. One of them will be here tomorrow morning," said Mr. Washington.

"Last weekend after they set the fire, they must have decided to lay low," said Nick.

"They knew suspicion would be up. That fire didn't set itself," said Mr. Washington.

"They left the drawing and the snake and the arrows?" asked Abby.

"Seems that way," said Mr. Washington.

"Every time you kids went into the woods, you cut into their chances to investigate the mound," said Uncle Roy.

"So, we were helping all along," said Matthew.

"Well, I have to admit that they might have gotten what they came for if you kids hadn't been so bullheaded," said Mr. Charlie.

"Will they be charged with arson as well as the crime of digging up historical stuff?" asked Nick.

"Yes, and some other charges as well," said Mr. Washington.

"Do they have a record?" asked Nick.

Uncle Roy nodded. "Some trespassing and entering without permission charges—enough to get the task force interested."

"What about the chase in the boat, Mr. Washington. Didn't they shoot at us then? And what about ramming your boat?" asked Matthew.

"They shot into the air over our heads," said Mr. Washington, "which is still dangerous, by the way."

"But you had a rifle," said Nick.

"I did. Always be prepared, Nick. Always expect the unexpected."

All three nodded.

"I couldn't believe when Abby flew out of the boat," said Matthew.

Abby smiled. "Me either."

Everyone laughed.

"That sure scared me when I heard about that," said Ms. Sarah.

"It didn't hurt me, Grandma. It was kind of exciting."

Ms. Sarah just shook her head. "You sure have an adventurous streak."

"Just like her dad," said Mr. Charlie.

"The shooting at Granddad was scarier to me than flying out of the boat," said Abby. Mr. Charlie reached down to pat her arm. She put her hand over his.

"They must have been getting desperate to ram us like that," said Mr. Washington.

"But the sheriff's boats were waiting for them anyway," said Nick.

"Yes, they were," said Uncle Roy.

"What about your boat, Herb?" said Mr. Charlie.

"My boat needs a little repair. I think the Sheriff's Department is going to help with that."

"You know, the mound is where I found that arrowhead," said Matthew. "At the edge of it where, I guess, those people had started digging. Do you think it's part of the artifacts of the burial?"

"Probably not, Matt," said Mr. Washington. "The items placed with the deceased would have been deeper in the ground. Also they would have been more personal and meaningful to the deceased than an arrowhead. But why don't you show it to Dr. Thibodaux tomorrow?"

"Who?" asked Matthew.

"He's an archeology professor I know from Centenary College," said Mom. "I took a Louisiana archeology course for teachers last summer that he taught. He's coming to take a look at the mound."

"And Bill Jones is coming too. Remember that author from the library talk? He's really excited to see the mound," said Ms. Sarah.

"Wow! Are they going to dig it up?" asked Nick.

"Two things required for that," said Mr. Washington. "One, they have to think it will offer information about the area that is not already known. Two, they must get permission from not only the State of Louisiana but also the Caddo Indian Nation."

"What about Matt's permission?" said Nick. "It *is* on his property."

"Well, my family's property," said Matthew.

"He already has our permission," said Mom.

"I wonder if they will use ground-penetrating radar to look

for buried artifacts?" said Nick. "They did at Poverty Point."

"That would be awesome to watch," said Matthew.

"Will they get back any of the artifacts that those people dug out of other historical sites?" Abby asked.

"We hope so," said Mr. Washington. "And the police hope to arrest the people who are receiving the stolen items. You may have helped break open a big case."

Matthew, Abby, and Nick beamed at each other.

"Yep. We are good at solving mysteries," said Nick. Everyone laughed.

Chapter 11
Saturday, June 21

The next morning, Matthew woke up to a knocking on the bedroom door. "Hey, fellas, wake up," said his mom. "Abby's here. Charlie brought us a surprise for breakfast."

Matthew got up and pulled on his blue jean shorts. "Nick. Nick. Come on," Matthew said as he shook Nick's shoulder and then pulled a tee shirt over his head.

Nick finally rolled over and sat up.

"Abby's here, Nick. I'm going. Hurry up and put on some clothes." Matthew headed out the bedroom door.

A wonderful smell hit him as he walked down the hallway. In the dining room Abby and Mr. Charlie were at the table, and sitting in the middle was a big pan of biscuits with a pint can of sugar cane syrup beside that.

"Matt, I told you I would find you some cane syrup," said Mr. Charlie. "Dig in. You're goin' to love it."

Mom was putting biscuits on plates and Matthew was passing them down the table as Nick walked into the room. "What's going on?" he asked, rubbing his eyes.

"Mr. Charlie brought us biscuits and syrup," said Kate.

"Biscuits and syrup? Why syrup?" asked Nick as he took a chair.

"It's like the sugar cane syrup that my great-grandparents made on this farm," said Matthew. "Mr. Charlie brought some for us to try."

Mr. Charlie showed them how to cut the biscuits in half and pour syrup over them. "You have to eat them with a fork. Can't pick these up like you do with jelly," he said.

"Wow, Mr. Charlie, this rocks," said Matthew. Nick stuffed his mouth with another bite of biscuit and nodded enthusiastically.

Uncle Roy nodded his head. "Haven't had any cane syrup since I was about Kate's age. Grandma used to give us biscuits and syrup. Have to admit that I had forgotten all about it."

"So my dad would have had this too?" asked Matthew as he took another bite.

"Yep," said Uncle Roy between bites. "You know, Matt, your dad would have been very proud of how you have handled yourself these last few days."

Mom smiled at Matthew and nodded her head in agreement.

Matthew thought about the hawk and the feeling of someone in the room with him. He was pretty sure that his dad had been with him all along. He smiled to himself and reached for another biscuit.

Matthew, Abby, and Nick hung out on the front porch after breakfast, waiting for the Indian mound experts to arrive. Around ten o'clock, a car crossed the cattle guard and pulled to a stop in front of the house. A tall man in overalls climbed out of the driver's seat while Mr. Jones got out of the passenger side of the car. Matthew opened the front door and called to his mom that the men had arrived. He then walked down the steps to welcome the men. Abby and Nick followed.

After introductions, Matthew said, "I wanted to show you these arrowheads, Dr. Thibodaux." He held out the box from the attic, and Abby opened her hand to reveal the arrowhead that Matthew had found in the mound.

Dr. Thibodaux took the box and used his finger to push the arrowheads around to look at them. Mr. Jones picked up the one in Abby's hand.

"This one is made of chert, typical for this area," said Mr. Jones, holding up the arrowhead that Matthew had found.

"What's chert?" asked Abby.

"It is a sedimentary quartz that formed after this area had been covered in sea life," explained Dr. Thibodaux.

"Oh, cool," said Nick, leaning forward to look closer at the stone of the arrowhead.

"This one looks like it is made from novaculite," said Dr. Thibodaux, holding up a gray arrowhead from the box. "That could indicate contact with tribes farther north in Arkansas or Oklahoma."

"Why is that?" asked Matthew.

"Novaculite is often found in the Ozark Mountains," answered Dr. Thibodaux.

"Like around Hot Springs?" asked Nick.

Dr. Thibodaux nodded. "Where were these arrowheads found?" he asked.

"We don't know for sure since they were found by my grandfather," said Uncle Roy as he joined the group. He shook hands with the men. "We assume they were from the pasture he cleared over there," he said, pointing to the pine woods, "or in that area where he raised sugar cane." He directed their attention to the woods north of the house.

"This one was at the edge of the Indian mound that we found," said Matthew, indicating the arrowhead that Mr. Jones held.

Matthew's mom and Kate joined the group. "Hello, Dr. Thibodaux."

"I'm so glad that you called me, Andrea. Now where is this mound?" asked Dr. Thibodaux, looking around at the group.

"It's in the pine trees, closer to the lake," answered Matt.

"We'll show you," said Nick.

As the group walked across the yard toward the pine trees, Dr. Thibodaux praised the kids for their smart handling of the Indian mound. "This mound just reaffirms the community of Caddo Indians in this area. You were a big help."

"Looks like I have found the topic of my next social studies project," said Nick, turning to Nick and Abby. "The Caddo Indians in Northwest Louisiana."

"Watch out, Nick," said Abby. "You might have to read some books." Matthew laughed at her comment.

"I think I just might be able to do that," replied Nick, smiling.

Acknowledgments

I wish to thank Judy Christie for her wonderful help and encouragement for this first novel. I would also like to thank two special friends who read and commented on early editions of the book. And, of course, I thank my family who read, copied, photographed, and did other various jobs to help me finish this project.

Author's Note

The Caddo Indians were a strong force in northwest Louisiana, northeast Texas, southwest Arkansas, and southeast Oklahoma. Not much of this land is now in the possession of these indigenous inhabitants. The focus of this novel is specifically on those who lived in northwest Louisiana. I have been told that the Caddo Indians may not have been the first residents of this area. You can find displays and evidence of the Caddo presence at several places, including the Adai Indian Nation Cultural Center in Robeline, Louisiana; the Caddo Mounds State Historic Site in Alto, Texas; and the Caddo Nation Caddo Heritage Museum in Binger, Oklahoma.

In the novel, the character Nick says that he has visited the Poverty Point World Heritage Site in Pioneer, Louisiana, to view the Indian mounds, but Nick had a distorted view of Native Americans as people. Perhaps Matthew was correct when he said that Nick had watched too many western movies. The good news is that Nick, as well as Abby and Matthew, learned that Mr. Washington was not a stereotype when they had a chance to spend some time with him. He quickly became their friend. This is how we get to know each other and different cultures, spending time together and giving other ideas a chance. It can be so interesting and there's so much to learn.

Perhaps, like Nick, your next history project could be on the first inhabitants of Louisiana. With a visit to your local library, you will find numerous books on these topics. (Louisiana libraries have special Louisiana sections. All those books already collected for you in one spot.) The internet is also a great resource; just be sure to verify your sources. Get researching!